"One night," Achilles said in that bare-bones voice, all his seductive techniques deserting him, leaving only demand.

"That's all I will ever ask of you. And I can tell you this with absolute confidence, that if you want to enjoy your first time with a man, then I am the man you should enjoy it with."

Silence.

"That's the most arrogant thing I've ever heard anyone say," Willow said at last.

He wanted to smile, but not because he was amused. "I have never pretended to be anything other than what I am. And yes, I can be arrogant at times. But if you know my reputation, then you will also know that women do not leave my bed unsatisfied." He felt wound tight as a spring. "I will make it a night to remember. I promise you."

Yet more silence, longer this time.

"Just one night?" she said at last. "One night and that's all?"

He didn't move. "Yes. One night and that's all."

The silence this time felt like the longest stretch of time he'd ever experienced.

"All right." Her voice was breathless. "You can have a wedding night."

Jackie Ashenden writes dark, emotional stories with alpha heroes who've just gotten the world to their liking only to have it blown apart by their kick-ass heroines. She lives in Auckland, New Zealand, with her husband, the inimitable Dr. Jax, two kids and two rats. When she's not torturing alpha males and their gutsy heroines, she can be found drinking chocolate martinis, reading anything she can lay her hands on, wasting time on social media or being forced to go mountain biking with her husband. To keep up-to-date with Jackie's new releases and other news, sign up to her newsletter at jackieashenden.com.

Books by Jackie Ashenden

Harlequin Presents

Crowned at the Desert King's Command
The Spaniard's Wedding Revenge
The Italian's Final Redemption

The Royal House of Axios

Promoted to His Princess
The Most Powerful of Kings

Shocking Italian Heirs

Demanding His Hidden Heir
Claiming His One-Night Child

Visit the Author Profile page
at Harlequin.com for more titles.

Jackie Ashenden

THE WORLD'S MOST NOTORIOUS GREEK

HARLEQUIN®
PRESENTS®

Recycling programs
for this product may
not exist in your area.

ISBN-13: 978-1-335-40393-3

The World's Most Notorious Greek

Copyright © 2021 by Jackie Ashenden

All rights reserved. No part of this book may be used or reproduced in
any manner whatsoever without written permission except in the case of
brief quotations embodied in critical articles and reviews.

This is a work of fiction. Names, characters, places and incidents
are either the product of the author's imagination or are used fictitiously.
Any resemblance to actual persons, living or dead, businesses,
companies, events or locales is entirely coincidental.

This edition published by arrangement with Harlequin Books S.A.

For questions and comments about the quality of this book,
please contact us at CustomerService@Harlequin.com.

Harlequin Enterprises ULC
22 Adelaide St. West, 40th Floor
Toronto, Ontario M5H 4E3, Canada
www.Harlequin.com

Printed in U.S.A.

THE WORLD'S MOST NOTORIOUS GREEK

CHAPTER ONE

WILLOW HALL HAD never seen a naked man before. Or at least, not one that wasn't on her computer screen when she'd inadvertently looked up the wrong thing on the internet. And definitely not coming boldly out of the lake he'd been swimming in only moments before, as if he didn't much care if there was anyone around to see him or not.

Of course, given the fact that the lake was on the Thornhaven estate's grounds and therefore private property, he probably wouldn't expect there to be someone lurking in the undergrowth at the lake's edge watching him.

Then again, this *was* private property and, even though Thornhaven had been vacant for the past few months following the old owner's death, it was clear that he was trespassing.

Not that it made her invasion of his privacy any less egregious, and not that she was technically any less a trespasser than he was, but still. She lived next door to the estate and had been walking the grounds for years, had played in the woods nearby as a child, had loved the overgrown, rambling nature of the estate ever since she could remember, and, even though it wasn't actually her property, she viewed it as such.

She'd certainly never expected to come across someone swimming in the lake when she'd set out blackberry picking this morning, still less swimming *naked*.

She should really do the right thing and move on. Visit the groundskeeper and tell him that there was a stranger in the lake. She really shouldn't be standing here peering through the trees like some pervert in an anorak.

Yet she didn't move.

Something held her rooted to the spot. Because the water was cascading over his naked body as he stepped from the lake, the late morning summer sun gilding his already golden skin, making an art form of every chiselled muscle. He was tall, with broad shoulders and lean hips. Long, powerfully muscled legs. His chest and stomach looked as if they'd been carved from marble as an example of the perfect masculine form, all hard planes and perfect hollows.

His hair was black, slick as a seal's, and as he walked slowly out of the water he lifted his hands and pushed it back from his forehead, biceps flexing with the movement.

Oh, lord…

Willow's mouth went dry, an inexplicable heat creeping through her, making her cheeks burn. This was very wrong. It wasn't the kind of thing she did at all. Maybe once, back when she'd been a teenager and much more prone to the vagaries of curiosity and her own wild passions, she wouldn't have thought twice about it, but certainly not now.

She was twenty-five, for God's sake, and she'd put those days behind her.

Yet somehow her feet wouldn't move, and she found she was clutching on to her basket full of blackberries, her fingers itching with the unfamiliar need to touch him, to trace the lines of all those intriguing muscles just to make sure he was real, because surely someone that beautiful couldn't be. She'd certainly never seen a man like this one, still less met anyone who looked the way he did, not in the cafe where she worked in Thornhaven village, or indeed anywhere in the village, full stop.

This man was like one of the Greek sculptures in her father's books on art history, the very pinnacle of male beauty, except all that travertine marble had been made flesh.

She didn't move, forgetting to breathe, the sunlight lovingly following every flex and release of his muscles as he bent over the small pile of clothes lying on the gravelly beach. He picked up a dark blue T-shirt then, as he straightened, Willow's heart beat even faster as he began to towel himself roughly off.

Her gaze drifted lower, over his lean hips and muscled thighs, to that most male part of him…

Her cheeks were so hot they felt scalded.

She should definitely *not* be looking at that.

What she should be doing was getting back to the cottage she lived in with her father, because she didn't like to leave him for too long. He'd had a stroke nine years ago that had left him extremely physically limited and very much dependent on her. Which he hated. But there was nothing either of them could do about that since there was no one else to look after him. She was his sole caregiver and it was a duty she took extremely seriously.

So she needed to stop staring and move on.

He'd started wiping down that incredible chest, his head bent, his profile as perfect as the rest of him. High forehead and straight nose. Cheekbones to die for and a strong, square jaw. His mouth was beautifully shaped and sensual, curving slightly, as if he knew something very wicked and utterly delightful…

Curiosity tightened inside her and she wanted very much to know what that something was.

Weren't you supposed to move on?

Yes, that was exactly what she'd been going to do. And she would. Right now.

'You'll get a better view from over there,' the man said casually, nodding at the bank directly in front of him.

Willow froze. His voice was as deep and rich as textured velvet, his accent aristocratic and yet with a lilt that suggested he'd spent a lot of time in places other than England. It tugged at something inside her, something she hadn't known was there.

She ignored the sensation, staying very still. He couldn't be talking to her, surely? She was hidden by the bushes and there was no way he could have spotted her. He hadn't even looked in her direction.

Perhaps he was talking to someone else. Someone

she hadn't seen. Or maybe he was talking on his phone. But no, that was stupid. He'd just come out of the lake and, given his current level of nakedness, it was very obvious he wasn't carrying a phone.

'It was your hair, by the way,' he went on, unhurriedly bending once again to the small pile of clothes and picking up a pair of plain black boxer shorts. 'If you were wondering what gave you away. It's very bright. I would suggest covering it with a scarf or hat next time you want to hide in the bushes and spy on someone.'

Oh, dear. He *was* talking to her.

A tide of intense embarrassment washed over her, heating her entire body in a way she hadn't felt for years. It made her feel as if she were a kid again, helpless shame filling her as her father spoke to her in that cold, quiet voice. The voice he only used when she'd done something wrong.

You have done something wrong. You intruded on this man's privacy.

A quick, bright anger at herself flickered inside her, and she caught her breath at the unexpected heat of it. But no. She wasn't going to get angry. That wouldn't help. Her emotions were dangerous things and she needed to keep her distance from them.

What she had to do now was own up to her indiscretion, give him an apology, then promise that it would never happen again.

Willow took a silent breath, forcing down the hot tangle of unwanted emotion that sat in her gut, then stepped out from behind the bush.

The beautiful man straightened, still naked, T-shirt

in one hand, his underwear in the other. He didn't seem at all embarrassed or self-conscious. Then again, he had nothing to be self-conscious or embarrassed about.

He was quite simply the most magnificent thing Willow had ever seen in her entire life.

His eyes were a deep, dark, midnight blue and the instant his gaze met hers she felt an almost physical impact, like a short, sharp electric shock. All the air left her lungs and her mind went utterly blank.

Then he smiled and she forgot where she was. She forgot *who* she was. Because that smile was warm and wicked and sensual all at the same time, and it made her feel hot and oddly feverish, though she had no idea why. She had no idea why a simple smile could do all those things to her.

He's dangerous.

The thought came out of nowhere, instinctive, though it didn't make any sense. Because he wasn't being threatening and she wasn't getting any strange vibes off him. He was simply standing there, smiling at her.

'Would you like to keep on looking?' Amusement glittered in his deep blue eyes. 'Or shall I dress?'

Willow struggled to get her brain working, her thought processes sluggish, as if they were mired in melted toffee. 'I do apologise,' she said in a scratchy voice. 'I heard the sounds of splashing and came to see what was happening.' Then, because, after all, he shouldn't be here, she added, 'You are aware that this is private property?'

The amusement in his eyes seemed to deepen. 'Oh,

yes, I'm aware. That is the whole point of trespassing, isn't it?'

So…this was deliberate? That didn't make any sense. Why would he deliberately break the law? Wasn't he worried that she would report him? But he didn't look worried. He didn't look worried about anything at all, which didn't seem fair. Especially when she felt as if she'd been struck by lightning.

She drew herself up to her not inconsiderable height, aware in the same moment that he was very much taller than she was, which didn't help her irritation. It didn't help either that he made not the slightest effort to cover himself or even dress.

'Well,' she said coolly, 'I suggest that you stop trespassing, get dressed, and leave the property. The groundskeeper here isn't very welcoming and he might decide to call the police.'

'Noted,' the man said, dry as dust. 'Are you the owner perhaps?'

'No. I'm the neighbour. I have permission.' Which was true. Her father and the previous owner of Thornhaven—the late Duke of Audley—used to be friends before the Duke had become a recluse, and they'd had an understanding about Willow's childhood rambles. It had suited her father to have her out of the house, because he found her a disruption.

'I see.' The man tilted his head, his eyes gleaming with an oddly wicked light. 'So have you finished looking?'

Willow's blush returned, though she ignored it as

fixedly as she'd ignored it the first time. If he could be perfectly calm about this, then so could she.

'Yes, I believe so.' She threw him a disapproving look. 'There's not much to look at after all.'

She expected him to be annoyed or even a little chagrined. He was not.

Instead, he laughed, and the sound hit her like a shock, wrapping around her, deep and dark as melted chocolate. And all she could think was that she'd never heard anyone laugh like that. In fact, it had been a long time since she'd heard anyone laugh at all.

'Far be it from me to disagree,' he said, 'but the blush in your cheeks would seem to indicate otherwise.'

Oh, yes, he's very dangerous.

That laugh of his was still resounding through her entire body, like she was a tuning fork he'd just struck, and she couldn't understand why. She couldn't understand her response to him at all. She only knew that some instinct inside her was urging her to get away from him and as quickly as possible.

However, Willow had given up listening to her instincts, because they were always wrong. And besides, running away would be to acknowledge that this man had got to her in some way, and she could never allow that.

'The blush in my cheeks has more to do with being suddenly accosted by a naked stranger than anything else,' she said. 'You could put on your shorts, you know.'

He raised one straight dark brow. 'You could also turn around.'

Willow ignored the burning in her cheeks. 'It's a bit late for that now, isn't it?'

'Indeed.' The glitter of amusement in his eyes changed, shifting into something else, something more intense. 'In that case you won't mind if I take my time about it.' He tilted his head again and, though his gaze didn't move from her face, she felt as if he'd scanned every inch of her body. 'Feel free to resume blackberry picking. Or you could stay and watch me dress. Either isn't a problem for me.'

She opened her mouth to tell him that she certainly wouldn't be staying, but he didn't wait for her to respond, instead turning and going over to where a pair of black running shorts and expensive-looking running shoes sat. Then he began to dress in an unhurried fashion.

His movements had an athletic grace to them that held her oddly mesmerised and she realised after a couple of moments that, far from resuming her blackberry picking as she'd fully intended, she was in fact standing there doing exactly the opposite.

This was ridiculous.

'I'm going now,' she announced, both to herself and to him.

He didn't respond, bending to tie the laces of his running shoes, black hair gleaming in the sun.

Yet her feet wouldn't move. It was as if her body had a mind of its own and what it wanted was to stay near him, which made no sense whatsoever. She'd had a couple of crushes on boys back in high school, but not since. She didn't have either the time or the inclination for such things, not when her primary focus was looking after her father and earning enough money to cover their expenses. That was far more important than mooning over some man, so why she was still here, fascinated by this particular man, she had no idea.

He rose again, his T-shirt still in one hand. He made no move to put it on and when he turned to face her, his incredible golden body still mostly on show, he didn't smile.

And all of a sudden Willow was certain that the danger she'd sensed from him before was about to make itself known and bizarrely, instead of fear, a sensation that felt a lot like excitement curled through her.

You know this is wrong. Walk away.

But the air between them was thickening with the strangest kind of tension. Hot and electric, like the atmosphere just before a summer storm.

She needed to leave, get away from him and his disturbing presence. Get away from the rush of what should not be excitement that crowded in her throat and from the fluttering in her stomach that felt like the wings of a thousand butterflies all beating at once. Get away from this physical response that she knew was wrong and bad for her, yet could not ignore, no matter how hard she tried.

But she didn't move. She stayed exactly where she was.

He started towards her like a great panther stalking its prey, moving with purpose, approaching her without any hesitation, coming so close that she could see drops of water glistening on his skin where he hadn't finished drying himself. She could smell, too, the fresh scent of the lake on him, undercut with something warmer, spicier and deeply masculine.

Her breath caught. Did men always smell this good or was it just him?

He was so tall she had to tilt her head back to look at him, which she couldn't recall ever having to do with anyone before.

'Look at you.' His deep voice was soft and warm with a familiarity that held her rooted to the spot. 'You have leaves in your hair.' He reached up and she was powerless to stop him as he casually extracted something from the tangle down her back. 'You also look like Diana, the huntress—did you know that?' He extracted another leaf. 'What were you hunting, Diana? Was it me, hmm? Well, you can stop your hunt now. You've caught me.' Then without any hesitation he slid the fingers of one hand into her hair and closed them into a fist, holding her firmly but very gently, the slight pressure making her tilt her head back ever further.

Willow was absolutely transfixed, her heartbeat so loud she couldn't hear anything else. Couldn't see anything else but the midnight blue of his eyes.

She'd never been touched like that before. Never had a man stand so close she could feel his heat, smell his warm, spicy scent. Never had strong fingers in her hair, carefully securing her.

Hunger rose inside her, forbidden and hot and desperate, though for what she had absolutely no idea.

But he seemed to know. Because he murmured,

'Time to take your trophy, my huntress.' Then leaned down and covered her mouth with his.

Achilles Templeton, Seventh Duke of Audley and known throughout the gossip columns of the world simply as Temple, was used to kissing women he didn't know.

He'd done it many times before, and it was always a pleasure. Women in general were always a pleasure and he made very sure they also thought the same of him. But he generally kept his attentions to socialites and party girls, experienced women who knew exactly who he was and what they were getting themselves into with him.

Not complete strangers wandering his estate grounds with leaves in their hair after being caught spying on him swimming.

In fact, he wasn't sure what had made him kiss this particular stranger.

If she'd caught him while running, he might have blamed it on the adrenaline high. But he hadn't been on an adrenaline high as he'd come out of the water. No, if anything he'd been cold as ice. It was his usual state, his cool control firmly in place, as it had been since he'd arrived at Thornhaven early that morning to tidy up his father's affairs.

But there were a lot of old ghosts in the old manor house and so he'd decided on exercise to get rid of them, going out for a run almost as soon as he'd arrived. But even twenty miles and a swim in Thornhaven's icy lake hadn't done a single thing to shift the dread inside him, the dread that had gripped him the minute he'd crossed the threshold. A dread that even cool distance couldn't shift.

It had only been the woman who'd provided the distraction he'd craved.

He'd caught a glimpse of her bright hair as he'd come out of the water and had been amused at how she'd tried to stay hidden. Because there was no hiding that brilliant shade of gold, not in amongst all that green.

Then all his amusement had vanished as she'd stepped out from behind the trees.

Tall, statuesque, her hair hanging down her back in a tangle all the shades of blonde and tawny, burnt toffee and gold, gilt and even a few streaks of silver. Her face was vivid, her features a mesmerising combination of sensual and girl-next-door, and her eyes were the intense golden brown of fine topaz. What she was wearing, he afterwards couldn't recall.

What he did know was that she was a golden goddess of a woman and the way she was looking at him was as if she'd never seen anything like him in all her life, as if she was dying of heat and thirst, and he was icy cold water...

Women looked at him all the time with varying degrees of desire and avarice, but he couldn't remember being looked at with wonder and that had hit him like a punch to the gut.

It had melted the dread clean away.

He'd only meant to take the leaves out of her hair. At least, that was what he'd told himself as he'd stridden towards her, the chemistry between them crackling and snapping like fresh green logs on a roaring fire.

He hadn't meant to slide his fingers into that glorious tangle of hair. He hadn't meant to bend his head and cover that beautiful mouth with his.

By rights, she should have slapped his face and called the police. But she hadn't.

She hadn't even moved. She'd just looked up at him, a hunger burning in her eyes and a question she probably didn't even know she was asking.

So he'd given her the answer. Without a single thought.

Her mouth was warm under his, but he could feel her tension. Could sense her shock. So he remained still, his lips gently resting on hers, his fingers curled around the silky mass of her hair. Waiting for her to either push him away or take it deeper.

A shudder went through her, as if she'd been fighting some internal battle and a part of her had surrendered. And her mouth softened under his, opening to let him in.

His fingers tightened in her hair as he tasted the tartness of blackberries and then something sweeter, like honey. Desire reached up inside him, gripping him by the throat, and he'd deepened the kiss before he was even conscious of doing so, exploring her mouth, chasing that delicious sweet yet tart taste.

She made a soft sound and he felt her fingers brush lightly, hesitantly over his chest. It felt as if a star had fallen and come to rest on his skin.

Theos, it burned. The touch centred him, grounded

him, got rid of the creeping sense of unreality that coming back to Thornhaven always seemed to inspire in him. The feeling of fading into nothing, becoming a ghost...

Suddenly the warm touch of her hand changed and it was no longer resting on his chest but pushing hard. Pushing him away.

He didn't want to let her go, because he knew if he did that feeling of fading away would return, but he'd never forced himself on anyone who didn't want him, so he made himself open his hands and let himself be pushed.

The glint in her eyes had gone molten, like liquid gold in the sunlight, and her cheeks were flushed. Her mouth was full and red, and he could see the fast beat of her pulse at the base of her throat.

'I...' she began in that rich, smoky voice, a thread of heat running through it. 'I...don't know... I can't...' She fell silent, breathing fast, staring at him.

Then before he could say anything she abruptly picked up the basket she'd dropped, turned and fled down the path that led around the lake.

Achilles stood very still, fighting the urge to go after her, catch her. Take her down on the forest floor and distract himself, ground himself in her lithe, strong body.

But his urges were always controlled and he didn't like how uncontrolled this one felt. Anyway, he never chased women, not when they came so easily to him, and so he wasn't about to start, no matter how much the idea appealed to him.

The neighbour, she'd said she was. Well, it wouldn't do to start off his tenure at Thornhaven by distressing the neighbour, now, would it?

He waited, breathing deeply, the hunger receding. He didn't know what he'd been thinking to kiss her like that. Clearly he'd let being back here at his family's estate get to him.

It wouldn't happen again, that was for sure.

He might be famous for his appetites, but his appetites were always controlled. He never let them rule him. He was the one who brought a woman to her knees, never vice versa.

Feeling more like his usual self, Achilles continued with his run back to the manor house.

Maybe he'd call up one of his favourite lovers and invite her to spend a weekend in the wild Yorkshire countryside. She probably wouldn't want to—Jess was a city girl through and through—but she did like having sex with him and that was a considerable inducement.

He was, after all, very, very good at it.

He'd nearly reached the house when his mobile went off. He didn't like to answer it when he was out running, but the sixth sense for trouble that had proved itself useful in his business life kicked in, so he stopped and pulled out his phone, glancing down at the screen.

It was Jane, his very efficient PA. Which meant it was probably something he needed to deal with.

He hit the answer button. 'What is it?'

'There's a problem with the will,' she said crisply,

getting straight to the point, which was what he liked about her.

Of course there was a problem with the will. When had his father ever given him anything but problems?

He stared out at the woods and moors that surrounded the manor house. 'Explain.'

'The lawyers have just got back to me. Apparently your ownership of the house is an issue. There are certain…codicils in the will that were overlooked.'

This was not a surprise. Even in death Andrew Templeton was still making sure to torture him.

'What are they?' he asked, part of him knowing already if not what those exact codicils would be, then certainly the intent of them.

'You must be married,' Jane said and then, uncharacteristically, hesitated.

Everything inside Achilles tensed. 'And?' he bit out.

Jane's voice when she spoke was quiet. 'And you must also have a son.'

CHAPTER TWO

A WEEK LATER, Willow was upstairs in her father's office giving it a good dusting. It was a small but cosy space at the back of the house, overlooking the little rose garden that she tried to maintain herself since her father hadn't been able to care for it following his stroke. It didn't look like much of a garden now, as she knew next to nothing about caring for roses. But she couldn't afford to employ a gardener, so it was that or nothing.

The straggly nature of the garden offended her sense of order, so she stopped looking out of the window, paying attention to the already dustless shelves of the office instead. Her father couldn't deal with stairs, meaning he was barely ever in here, which made dusting pointless, but she didn't like to see his office look unused so she kept it clean just in case.

Besides, she liked looking at his collection of books. Not so much his medical textbooks as the ones he had on botany that he kept for interest's sake. The woods outside had always held a fascination for her and so she liked reading about plants, or anything to do with the natural world. She had dreams every so often, of going to university and doing a science degree, studying Biology and Natural Sciences, but of course that was impossible.

Not when she barely earned enough to cover her and her father's existing expenses and maintenance for the old cottage, let alone for university fees. And then there was the ongoing issue of care for him. She could leave him alone for the day while she worked, but not longer than that.

She definitely wasn't able to leave him while she undertook a degree, though study by distance might be an option. But still there was the issue of fees.

It was a situation that both her and her father were unhappy with, but both of them were trapped in it and there wasn't much to be done.

She couldn't leave him alone. He was her father, and she owed it to him. Not only because he'd had to give up his career as a surgeon after his stroke, but also because he'd brought her up after her mother died, and that hadn't been easy. She'd been a difficult child, hard to manage even for the nannies he'd employed. Eventually he'd been forced to bring her up himself, which had greatly impacted on the career he'd wanted for himself—as he'd never ceased to point out to her.

It wasn't his fault that they had no money and the cottage was falling down around their ears. It wasn't his fault that he was limited in what he could do because she wasn't able to help him physically the way he needed her to.

It wasn't his fault that she'd basically ruined his life.

Willow knew all that. Just as she knew it was her job to fix it.

She frowned ferociously at her duster, her brain sorting through various money-making scenarios.

The extra shifts she'd picked up at the cafe would help, but they weren't a good long-term solution. No, she was going to have to think of something else.

Her phone in her jeans pocket buzzed.

She took it out and glanced at the screen, and saw a text from her father:

Come down to the sitting room.

Since his stroke had left him unable to walk with any ease, he'd taken to texting her when he needed her to do something for him. It was a system that worked very well, except when she was in the middle of doing something and he was impatient. But luckily those instances were few and far between.

Clarence Hall was where he usually was, sitting in his old armchair near the brick fireplace when she got downstairs, his handsome face drooping slightly on one side due to the effects of the stroke. He'd always been a stern, serious man who'd never had much time for humour, and today he seemed even more serious than usual.

'Sit down, Willow,' he said in sententious tones.

Willow checked—surreptitiously, because he hated it when she fussed—that he had what he needed on the table beside his chair, then sat in the armchair opposite. 'What is it, Dad?'

'I have some news.' He pulled at the edge of the checked woollen rug that covered his knees, seemingly agitated, which was very unlike him. 'Something that I haven't told you and should have.'

A curl of foreboding tightened inside her, but she ignored it. If her father hated her fussing, he hated her worrying more. In fact, he hated all excess emotion, and so Willow had spent many years curbing her wayward feelings and getting them under control.

She knew all too well the dangers when she let them run riot.

'That sounds portentous.' With the ease of long practice she schooled her brain into focus, because it tended to go off on tangents when she was supposed to be listening and her father got very annoyed when he thought she wasn't paying attention.

'That's because it is.' Her father gave her his usual repressive stare, as if he expected her to start screaming or weeping or performing any other such unwanted emotional display.

But Willow's last show of anger had been when she was sixteen and she had kept her feelings under perfect control since then, so she simply gave her father the same cool stare back.

He gave an approving nod. 'Well, you recall Audley, don't you? Who died a couple of months ago?'

Audley referred to the Duke of Audley, who owned Thornhaven and with whom her father had once been friends years earlier. He'd been a virtual recluse for nearly as long as Willow had been alive and that, coupled with her father's physical limitations, had meant it was a friendship very much in the past tense even before he'd died.

Reminded suddenly of Thornhaven, Willow caught her breath as yet again the memory of what had happened just over a week ago rushed to fill her head. Of the beautiful man coming out of the lake and of that kiss he'd given her.

Heat crept into her cheeks and she had to pretend she was examining a loose thread on the edge of the sofa cushion to hide it.

The memory of that wretched encounter kept creeping up on her whenever she least expected it, no matter that she'd put the entire incident from her mind the instant she'd fled. And there should be no reason to think of it now. None at all.

Briefly she'd debated contacting the groundskeeper to tell him she'd seen someone trespassing, but then the thought of being questioned about said trespasser made her feel uncomfortable and so she'd dismissed the idea. If that…person ever trespassed again, the groundskeeper would soon catch him, that was for sure.

'Yes, I remember Audley,' she said, forcing the memory away and trying to bring her attention back to her father. 'I don't think I met him though, did I?'

'No, you were too young. But the Duke and I talked often, or rather we used to. He became a recluse about ten years ago and I didn't see him at all after that.'

'That's probably why I didn't meet him then. Why do you want to know?'

Her father's dark eyes were still sharp and they gave her a very direct look. 'We made a certain…gentleman's agreement one night. It was a long time ago and I forgot about it. Especially when he broke off all contact. However…' Uncharacteristically, her father paused, seeming hesitant. 'I got a letter yesterday from the Duke's office, reminding me of the agreement and asking me to honour it.'

Willow frowned, unsure of where her father was going with this. 'What agreement? Please don't say it concerns money, because you know—'

'It's not about money,' Clarence interrupted, his voice flat.

The foreboding that she'd forced away earlier crept back, though she fought it down. 'Then what is it about?'

Her father's fingers picked at the edge of his blanket, yet more signs of an agitation that wasn't like him at all.

What have you done now?

The foreboding gripped her tighter, even though she hadn't done anything that would cause her father grief, not recently at least.

That kiss maybe?

She swallowed. No, surely not? Who would have told him? No one else had been at the lake, she was sure of it. And anyway, what did that kiss have to do with the Duke of Audley?

'Audley and I went to university together,' her father said. 'This was before I married, but he'd just come home from Greece with his new wife, and she was pregnant. They knew it was a boy. We were celebrating his impending fatherhood and he suggested that if I was to ever have a daughter, then she could marry his son. I…confess I'd had more than a couple of pints and I was a little worse for wear. I agreed that it was a fine idea and so we shook on it. He never mentioned it again and neither did I, and soon I forgot about it.'

Willow blinked in surprise. She couldn't imagine her father drinking let alone being 'a little worse for wear'. He was famously abstemious and hated rowdiness of any kind. He also wasn't the type to indulge in drunken gentlemen's agreements either.

'I see,' she said, puzzled. 'So why are you mentioning this to me now?'

'Because the Duke of Audley's son, now the *current* Duke of Audley, has asked me to make good on my promise.'

Willow's surprise deepened. An arranged betrothal between the children of two friends lost in the mists of time? The idea was so ridiculous, so utterly preposterous, it had to be a joke. 'Dad, are you sure this isn't a scam? Is the letter legitimate?'

'Yes, of course it's legitimate and I know a scam when I see one.' His mouth thinned. 'The Duke wishes to see you tomorrow night at Thornhaven so he can put his proposal to you.'

She opened her mouth. Shut it again. She didn't know whether to laugh at the insanity of the situation or be outraged by it. But, since she didn't display any extremes of emotion these days, she settled on a tight smile. 'I appreciate the invitation obviously, but he can't possibly think that I'm going to agree to it.'

But Clarence only stared at her. 'He has offered certain…financial incentives.'

Oh. No wonder her father was taking this so seriously.

She was very conscious all of a sudden that her palms were damp and her heartbeat had quickened. 'What kind of financial incentives?' she asked, pleased by how level she sounded.

'I don't know,' her father said, his gaze still sharp and direct. 'His letter was very brief. I assume he'll tell you more when you meet him.'

She stiffened. 'What do you mean, "when"? I'm not going to Thornhaven—'

'I want you to hear him out, Willow,' Clarence said flatly. 'We can't keep going on the way we have.'

'But I've taken on extra shifts—'

'That's not going to help either of us and you know it.' Her father's expression became hard, the way it always did when he thought she was disobeying him. 'The house needs to have money spent on it, or we need to sell it. I've been looking into treatment for myself too. There are a couple of options that would improve my quality of life immensely, but they're expensive. And I'm tired of waiting. This could be the answer, Willow.'

It was true. Depending on what kind of 'financial incentives' the Duke was offering, it could mean the solution to all their difficulties.

And all she'd have to do was marry a complete stranger.

You wanted to fix this. You're the reason you're in this mess in the first place, after all.

That was also true. Her father might have been a

world-renowned surgeon if her mother hadn't wanted a baby and hadn't talked her father into it; he hadn't been keen on the idea. And if her mother hadn't then died six months later in a car accident, leaving her grieving father to bring up a child he hadn't wanted in the first place. An overly emotional, stubborn and headstrong child, whom her reserved and self-contained father had no idea what to do with. And whose behaviour had been a contributing factor in the stress that had triggered his stroke.

She swallowed down the guilt, forced it aside along with all the other unwanted emotions that still seethed inside her, no matter how many years she'd spent ignoring them. Once, she'd thought that they'd go away altogether, or at least she wouldn't feel them so very deeply, but that day hadn't come yet.

When she'd been very young and her father's disapproval and cold distance had been too much for her, she'd used to escape into the woods and the Thornhaven estate, where she could shout and sing and even scream to herself and no one would tell her to be quiet or to go away, or that she was a damn nuisance.

But she didn't go into the woods often these days, because these days she was much better at controlling herself. She wasn't that difficult child any more.

'In that case,' she said without inflection, 'Of course I'll see him.'

Her father gave her another of his sharp, assessing looks, as if he'd somehow picked up a note of protest in her tone, though there hadn't been even the faintest hint of one. 'You don't have to marry him, Willow. No one's going to force you. It's not the Middle Ages after all. But the logical thing to do is to get all the information so you can make an informed decision.'

She didn't know how he'd managed to pick up on her reluctance, not when she'd barely acknowledged it herself. Or perhaps it wasn't reluctance, only surprise due to the unusual nature of the request.

Whatever, her father was right. She needed to gather all the information before making a decision, in which case accepting the Duke's invitation was the logical thing to do.

Really, she was viewing this with far too much emotion, especially when she didn't even know what kind of proposal the Duke was going to put forward.

It clearly wasn't going to be a real marriage, not when they'd never met. Perhaps it was because of some legal difficulty? Not that it mattered. Marriage—whenever she thought of it, which she seldom did—seemed to work well for some people, but it required a certain amount of emotional involvement that she wasn't willing to give.

She would have to inform the Duke of that when they met so he was clear. She certainly wouldn't want to mislead anyone.

'No, you're right,' she said in the same cool tone. 'You can tell the Duke that I'd be happy to accept his invitation.'

Her father was pleased, she could tell, and that gave her a certain satisfaction. And, since she wasn't going to get anything done if she thought about it too much, she put it out of her mind.

At least until the next day rolled around and she couldn't put it out of her mind any longer.

She told herself that she wasn't in the least bit nervous as she surveyed her very meagre wardrobe, trying to decide on what to wear. She never went out anywhere, so she didn't have any nice dresses apart from a summery cotton thing in white. She liked the dress, but putting it on made her feel as though she was making an effort and some stubborn part of her didn't want to be seen to be making an effort.

The same stubborn part of her that had refused to look up anything about the current Duke of Audley on the web. There was bound to be something about him—some photos at least—to give her an idea about what to expect, but something inside her absolutely refused.

She knew that giving in to her stubborn streak wasn't a good idea, since it had caused her problems in the past, but she rationalised it, by telling herself that she didn't want to go to Thornhaven with any preconceived ideas.

Besides, she'd find out about him soon enough, and there was always the possibility that the whole ridiculous situation was a joke. Or something her father had misunderstood, or some other easily explicable thing that would become apparent the moment she arrived.

It wouldn't have anything to do with her actually marrying some man she'd never met, and a duke at that.

So she didn't make an effort. She wore jeans and a serviceable shirt in plain white and she didn't even touch her very likely out-of-date make-up. She made sure her father had everything he needed for the evening, double-checked his phone was within reach so he could call her if he had to, and then she stepped outside and walked across the lawn to the little path that would take her to Thornhaven.

It was a beautiful evening, the long summer twilight lying over the moors beyond the woods lighting the grey stone of the large, Georgian manor house. Ivy covered the walls, softening the stark, square lines and the austere front entrance.

While Willow loved Thornhaven's grounds—its wild wood and large ornate gardens—she'd never actually been in the house itself.

But she'd always been curious about it. When she'd been much younger and wilder, she'd made up stories in her head about the reclusive Duke who lived there, fairy tales where the Duke became a dark and dangerous prince who was rescued and led to redemption by the girl who lived next door, who was also a princess with super-powers.

Those were ridiculous stories though, and ones she'd left behind long ago.

Now as she approached the front entrance, her footsteps crunching over the gravel of the driveway, she wasn't thinking about fairy tales, but why the old Duke had been a recluse. And why his son hadn't visited him. Why that son had been in touch with her father to call in this ridiculous gentleman's agreement. Not to mention why he hadn't contacted her directly.

Nerves fluttered inside her as she stopped in front of the big front door and pressed an incongruously modern-looking button for the doorbell set in the door frame.

The door was immediately opened by a slightly cadaverous-looking man who was clearly one of the Duke's staff. He greeted her, requested that she follow him, then, without waiting for a response, stalked off, leaving Willow no choice but to do what he said.

She wasn't given time to look around, though she caught a glimpse of high ceilings and ornate plasterwork, and paintings in heavy gilded frames. The floor was worn parquet and her footsteps scuffed as she hurried after the staff member who was obviously doing butler duties.

He opened a door to her left and ushered her into a very comfortable sitting room with a huge fireplace down one end, where a collection of couches and armchairs were arranged in front of it. Bookshelves stood against the white panelled walls, piled high and untidily with vast amounts of books. There were occasional tables scattered about and littered with various knickknacks, piles of papers, more abandoned books, plus a few cups and saucers. Old silk rugs covered the floor, softening the stark feel of the place, but nothing could mask the faint smell of must and damp. The scent of an old, neglected house that had been shut up and abandoned for far too long.

Despite that, the sitting room gave the impression of a room well lived-in, and it was warm, and Willow found herself relaxing somewhat.

'The Duke will be with you directly,' the man said

and left without another word, closing the door behind him.

Willow stood a moment, the silence of the house settling around her. Out of the corner of her eye she spotted a small painting near the fire that looked suspiciously like a Degas, but surely couldn't have been. And she was just starting towards it to have a closer look, when she heard the door open again behind her, then close just as quietly.

And all the hairs on the back of her neck lifted in a kind of primitive awareness.

'Hello Diana,' a deep, rich and very familiar male voice said.

Willow Hall, daughter of his father's old friend Clarence Hall, stood near the fireplace with her back to him, her hair flowing down her spine just as wild and glorious as it had it been beside the lake the week before.

Though this time there were less leaves in it.

Achilles waited, anticipation gathering tightly inside him.

After Jane had informed him of the will bombshell, he'd spent an intense and very expensive couple of days with his legal team examining every inch of the document and its codicils, trying to find any loopholes. But there were none. His father had left nothing to chance. The Thornhaven estate could only legally be owned by him if he married and had a son.

Really, he should have expected more hoops to jump through, but he'd thought his father would have long since forgotten his existence, since Achilles had purposely forgotten his. A stupid thought, clearly. Or perhaps his father expected him to be grateful?

Regardless, he'd spent the past fifteen years of his life making sure the world and everyone in it knew that Achilles Templeton was his own man and had nothing to do with his historic lineage. That he was vastly successful and a force to be reckoned with, in his own right.

He'd built a billion-dollar high-risk venture-capital firm from nothing, using only his excellent brain and his business skills and, not only that, but was the scourge of the elite party circuit as well. He worked hard, played harder, and if his life was one of excess, it was an excess he'd earned.

And if he took a great amount of satisfaction that the name 'Templeton' had become synonymous with a certain dissolute lifestyle, then what of it? Achilles didn't care. His father certainly wouldn't, because his father had never cared what Achilles did.

But apparently his father had cared. In the last few years of his life he'd somehow remembered he had a son and that said son was going to inherit the title when he died, so naturally enough, in a last, spiteful gesture, old Andrew Templeton had made sure that inheritance was as difficult for Achilles to get his hands on as possible.

Because of course, in his father's eyes, it wasn't Achilles' inheritance at all.

It was his brother's. Who'd died years ago.

Perhaps the old man was expecting Achilles to

give up and let him have the last laugh. Achilles certainly didn't need the money or the title, or the austere, gloomy manor house that went with it. He'd bought property in Greece, his mother's country, and spent most of his time going from one country to another, following his business interests and the parties that went along with them, and certainly didn't have any ties to his father's country. He had no loyalty to the title, felt no need to settle down and continue the bloodline. Domestic bliss was the last thing he wanted. And there was a comfortable, reassuring emptiness in his heart where sensations of an emotional nature should have been, and weren't, that he was in no hurry to fill.

Yet the moment Achilles heard about the will's requirements, it was as if someone had flicked a switch on inside him. That emptiness in his heart had rippled and shifted, currents moving inside him, and he realised that yes, he in fact *did* care about this. And no, his father would *not* have the last laugh.

The house and the title were his and he would have both, and if his father thought that marriage and fatherhood would be enough to put him off, the old bastard was wrong.

Then after the codicil had been discovered, his lawyers had found something else in amongst his father's documents.

Written down on a very old piece of paper and signed by both parties was an agreement that promised the Seventh Duke of Audley, one year and two months old at the time, to the yet-to-be-born oldest daughter of Dr Clarence Hall. The agreement was dated long enough in the past that it was clear the Seventh Duke of Audley was, in fact, Achilles' dead older brother, Ulysses, who'd died of meningitis when he was fifteen.

His older brother who somehow in death was more alive than Achilles had ever been in life.

It was clear from the will that his father hadn't wanted Achilles to inherit everything that should have been Ulysses'. Which meant, of course, that Achilles had to do everything in his power to take what should have been his older brother's and make it his own.

Including Ulysses' intended bride.

His father would have turned in his grave if he knew Achilles was intended to step into precious Ulysses' shoes, but Achilles didn't care. That was what he wanted. The old man had denied him everything as a child and he could pretend that didn't matter to him now, that he was long since over the neglect and pain caused by both his parents. But it did matter. He was over the pain, but maybe the anger was still there.

So he'd got his legal team to look into the document and to research this Clarence Hall, and, sure enough, they'd turned up a daughter. Except she'd been born many years after Ulysses' death and a good ten years after his own birth, too. Clearly his father had forgotten about the agreement and had done nothing about it since, but it appeared that the girl—or rather woman now—lived with her father and had remained unmarried.

Which had been all to the good. And then his team had handed him a photo of Miss Willow Hall, and it had felt as if he'd been struck by lightning.

Because it turned out that the woman he'd kissed by the lake the week before was the same woman.

Which made everything crystallise in his head.

That lovely, lovely woman would be his wife and together they would make the most beautiful child. He would have the inheritance his father had denied him, and she would make it a pleasure to do so.

Ulysses' intended bride would be his, the final repudiation of everything his father stood for.

The old Duke had thought to leave him a curse, but instead he'd given Achilles a gift.

So he took it.

He'd pored over the information his team had provided for him, investigating every aspect of Willow Hall's life. Which wasn't much. She worked at the cafe in the village while caring for her father, who'd had a stroke nine years earlier. Her finances—because of course he investigated those—were in a terrible state, since she didn't get paid much and obviously couldn't get work elsewhere because of her father's health.

She was in dire straits and, as he was a man who'd built his business empire by taking advantage of every opportunity that came his way, he would take advantage of this one too.

Money would be the lever he'd pull in order to get her to do what he wanted, since money he had in abundance. Sex too was a lever, as he knew after that encounter down by the lake that she wanted him. Not that it would be any hardship; there was nothing he liked more than making a woman burn for him.

No, he'd always come second to the dead brother

he'd never met, but he wouldn't any longer. Ulysses was dead, but Achilles wasn't, and he would have what was rightfully his.

Willow had gone very still, like a deer catching a predator's scent.

He'd thought she'd have researched him before she'd arrived the way he had with her, and would already know that he was the man she'd met by the lake. But it was clear from her stiff posture and sudden tension that she hadn't known. Not until he'd spoken.

He stared at her elegant back, conscious of desire stirring to life almost instantly inside him.

Ah yes, he remembered that feeling, not to mention his own uneasiness with the ferocity of it. But he could manage that. It was only physical desire, and he knew, if anyone did, that desire only meant what you wanted it to mean. Which to him was only pleasure, nothing more. There was nothing emotional about it. Emotions he avoided like the plague.

So he let himself look at her, let the desire rise inside him, because she was tall and sleek, and her figure was accentuated by the plain jeans and white shirt she wore. And her blonde hair was falling down her back in a simple ponytail caught at the nape of her neck, and she was still every bit the wild goddess she'd been in the woods that day.

She would be a perfect wife for him, at least for a time. And the perfect mother for their child. It was as if she'd been intended for him all along, and their intense chemistry only proved it.

'Except your name isn't Diana, is it?' he murmured into the silence. 'It's Willow. Willow Hall.'

She turned around abruptly, her gaze the same brilliant golden brown as he remembered, and just as full of shock.

Then the sexual tension hit, a sharp jolt of electricity that had him catching his breath.

Colour rose into her cheeks, making it clear that she felt it too, though he knew that already. He'd tasted her desire for him along with the tart hint of blackberry.

'You,' she breathed.

Achilles inclined his head. 'Yes. It is indeed. The naked man you kissed beside the lake last week.'

'You're…you're the Duke?'

'Achilles Templeton, Seventh Duke of Audley. My friends call me Temple.' He gazed at her vivid, passionate face. 'But I suppose you're probably wanting to call me "that bastard".'

'That's why you were swimming,' she said, ignoring him. 'You weren't trespassing.'

'No.' He shook his head slowly. 'I was out for a run and decided to cool off in the lake. *My* lake.'

She kept on staring, her eyes wide. Then the shock drained away and a thousand angry golden sparks glittered suddenly in her gaze. She strode forward, closing the space between them without hesitation until she stood only inches away.

The expression on her face now blazed with outrage and anger. A goddess who'd been wronged and who was now looking to punish some poor worshipper for their transgression.

Theos, but she was magnificent. So tall he barely had to tilt his head to meet her gaze, and her anger had brought the most beautiful flush to her golden skin.

There were very few people who confronted him in this way these days. He covered his single-mindedness and the icy streak of ruthlessness that ran through him with a veneer of dry amusement to put people at ease, which was useful when it came to both business and pleasure. But that veneer was thin. And when people sensed it, they were intimidated.

But she was not intimidated. She was not afraid. She looked at him as if she wanted to strike him for his temerity and he found that he almost wanted her to try. He would enjoy a fight with this woman. Anger was a potent fuel when it came to generating pleasure.

'How dare you?' She sounded shaken and furious, her eyes gone a smoky, molten gold. 'How dare you not even say one single word to me? You should have told me who you were, not let me assume. And how dare you let me come here not knowing—?'

'I didn't *let* you do anything,' he interrupted coolly, though cool was the last thing he felt. 'I assumed that you would have done the most basic internet search. Research, Diana. Isn't that what intelligent people do?'

He knew saying that would be like throwing a lighted match into a pool of spilled petrol, but he wanted to see her blaze. And she did. She went up like a torch.

He saw the moment her temper snapped, the moment her hand lifted, and so he was ready, grabbing her wrist calmly before her palm could connect with his cheek, the sound of his heartbeat roaring in his head.

You fool. What do you think you're doing, provoking her like this?

Maybe he was a fool. But now her skin was warm against his fingertips and her furious golden gaze was on his, staring right at him. And he realised he'd never felt more alive than he did in this moment. In this old house he hated, that somehow still managed to make him feel like a ghost in the walls, even all these years later.

A taut, crackling second passed.

Her skin was warm and silky, and he could feel the tension in her arm. Outrage and fury poured off her. She was like the sun during a solar flare, flames leaping in her eyes, a fire burning under her skin.

It made him want to take that fire in his hands and coax it higher, make it burn brighter. Turn it into a bonfire. And only when it was blazing as high as it would go would he step into the flames and have them consume them both.

Careful. She could have you on your knees.

No, she wouldn't. He'd never let anyone have power enough to put him on his knees and he certainly wasn't going to start with this woman, no matter how lovely she was.

In fact, maybe he should prove it. Both to himself and her.

Achilles firmed his grip on her wrist, then slid his other hand around the back of her neck, cupping her nape. Then he pulled her in and took her mouth.

She didn't pull away, didn't protest. A low moan escaped her instead that sounded a lot like relief, as a shudder coursed the length of her body. Her lips parted beneath his. She tasted of melted honey and wild heat, and before he knew what he was doing he'd deepened the kiss, his tongue exploring her mouth, his hand on the back of her neck holding her still.

Dimly, a part of him was appalled, because this wasn't how he'd intended this meeting to go. He was supposed to present her with his proposal, lay out his terms. Give her the details of her financial recompense, offer her some refreshments and then possibly, depending, offer her some sexual inducements as well. Not a full seduction, not yet, but certainly a reminder of their chemistry. Just enough to pique her hunger.

He was not supposed to kiss her again within seconds of being in her presence.

So much for her not having any power over you. You're about to take her right here and now.

The thought registered, a bright shock in his head. No, that was ridiculous. He was the one in control here.

Forcing away his desire, Achilles lifted his head. But he kept his grip on her wrist and his hand on the back of her neck, holding her where he wanted her. Testing his control still further, because obviously he needed the reminder.

Her eyes were molten honey, her mouth full and red. The pulse at the base of her throat raced and the pretty flush that stained her cheeks now extended down her neck and beneath her shirt.

She looked as dazed and as hungry as he felt.

'I would not advise getting close to me again.' He tried to make the warning sound casual and offhand, but his voice was rougher than he wanted it to be. 'Not if you don't want to end this with you on the floor and me inside you.'

She blinked, as if coming back to herself. Then just like that the hunger in her eyes vanished, the golden flames of her fury flooding back.

This time though she'd learned her lesson, because she jerked herself out of his grip and strode back to the fireplace then stopped, keeping her back to him.

The silence seethed and crackled, the tension drawn so tight it was almost a living presence.

But he had himself well in hand now and he didn't move.

'I apologise,' she said at last, her voice slightly shaky-sounding, her whole figure stiff with tension. 'I shouldn't...have done that.'

An apology? He wasn't expecting that. How...interesting.

Achilles put his hands in his pockets and studied her obdurate back. 'Shouldn't it be me apologising? I'm the one who kissed you. Which I'm not sorry for, by the way.'

'I'm not talking about the k-kiss. I was...going to hit you.'

Ah.

'Yes. I know you were.'

She turned around sharply, and for a second he saw real distress glittering in her eyes. 'I lost my temper and I shouldn't have.'

A slight discomfort twisted in his chest. He didn't like distressing a woman, especially a woman he was attracted to, and, though he didn't concern himself overmuch with other people's feelings, he wasn't a man who got pleasure out of pain.

'It wasn't entirely without provocation,' he allowed.

'But you're right.' She lifted her chin. 'I should have done my research. I should have at least prepared myself by looking up your name and I didn't.'

This was not going the way he had thought it would. He should have been pleased with her apology and then her admission, yet he felt vaguely...dissatisfied in some way. Almost as if he'd wanted her to fight more.

Not a good idea considering what just nearly happened.

No. Perhaps not.

'So why didn't you?' he asked.

'Because I...didn't want to.' The distress had disappeared, along with her anger, a certain cool dignity gathering about her. 'I'm only here because of that letter you wrote to my father and he thought I should hear you out.' Her gaze narrowed. 'Though I think you should know that I have no intention of marrying you.'

Achilles smiled. Because there were many things she didn't know about him, the most important being that he always got his way.

'Well,' he said mildly. 'Let's see if I can change your mind.'

CHAPTER THREE

HE WAS NOT going to change her mind, Willow had already decided that. There was nothing he could do, nothing he could say.

Not after she'd lost her temper and nearly slapped him.

Not after he'd answered that with a kiss that had made her forget everything, even her own name. A kiss she'd let him take, because she hadn't been able to help herself.

She was a fool. The minute she'd heard him speak, she should have walked out of the room. But she hadn't.

Instead, she'd heard his voice and turned around and seen him, the beautiful man from the lake. And, just like that moment a week earlier, she hadn't been able to move.

He'd been dressed this time, but that in no way had lessened his sheer physical impact. He wore a dark blue business shirt open at the neck that deepened the colour of his eyes and enhanced the breadth of his shoulders, as well as black suit trousers that emphasised his lean waist and powerful thighs.

And the very second he'd locked his intense blue gaze on her an electric pulse of desire had gone through her, shaking her down to her soul. Making her realise that her week of telling herself she'd forgotten all about him was a lie. That the memory of the kiss he'd stolen from her was seared into her brain. And worse: she wanted more.

And just as she was processing all of that, she'd become aware that he'd called her Diana before she'd turned around. Which meant he'd known who she was before she'd arrived.

Willow had thought she had her temper well under control these days. She hadn't lost it in years. But right then her grip on it had faltered and a wave of righteous fury had filled her, partly fuelled by shock at his presence and the fact that he'd known who she was, and partly by the shame of her own physical response.

So she'd stormed up to him, ready to give him a piece of her mind, and then he'd said that thing about intelligent people doing research, sounding so much like her father at his most dismissive that what little grip she had left on her temper failed completely.

Thoughtlessly she'd raised her hand, ready to slap his arrogant, handsome face, to do harm to another person. Then he'd grabbed her wrist and stopped her, kissing her, and all her anger had abruptly found a new path: desire.

She'd let herself get lost in that kiss, let it carry her away. Because for some inexplicable reason the way he held her, contained her, made her feel safe. As if she could rage inside the circle of his arms, push against him, fight him, and he would remain immovable.

She had no idea why she'd felt that way. She only knew that when he'd pulled away, all her anger had come rushing back and she'd had to jerk herself out of his arms and put as much distance between them as she could. Because he was right: getting close to him was dangerous.

You cannot marry him.

No, there was no way. Not when his very presence threatened her hard-won control over herself and her emotions. She couldn't allow herself to go back to the girl she'd been before her father's stroke, angry and stubborn and rebellious. Who made life difficult for everyone around her. Who hurt those she loved.

She trembled as the splinter of an old guilt tugged at her heart, but she forced it away. Forced *all* those terrible, awful emotions away.

She couldn't lose her temper again. She wouldn't.

The Duke was standing in the middle of the room, his hands in his pockets, his head tilted to one side. It was a relaxed, casual pose, and yet the way he looked at her was anything but casual. The deep midnight of his eyes burned and he radiated a subtle, sensual energy that made the air around him crackle.

He looked like a man who'd never heard the word 'no' in all his life.

Unluckily for him, 'no' was the only word she had.

'I'm not going to change my mind.' She clasped her shaking hands together in an effort to still them. 'I'm not marrying you.'

His gaze flickered, his mouth curving slightly, and she had the disturbing thought that far from putting him off, her insistence was only inciting him further.

'But you haven't heard my proposal yet,' he said mildly. 'Isn't that why you're here?'

'I don't need to hear it. I already know that my answer will be no.'

'Of course. But you can hardly tell your father that you heard me out when you haven't, in fact, heard me out.'

Oh, that was right, her father. The money. Treatments...

Willow swallowed, fighting a sudden wave of stupid panic. This was madness. Logic was the answer to this mess, not the wild swing of her emotions. She had to get herself under control and stop listening to her gut.

'Fair enough.' She tried to sound as level as possible. 'Let's hear your proposal, then.'

He didn't say anything though, his gaze holding hers, and she could feel the air between them thicken again, a charge building like static.

Why was it that every time she looked at him, all she could think about was how he tasted? How hot his mouth had been on hers? How wild and hungry for him she was...?

He smiled lazily, as if he could read her every thought. 'Some refreshments first, I think.'

Willow opened her mouth to tell him that she didn't want any refreshments, but he'd already turned to the door, moving over to it with that easy, athletic grace that she found hard not to notice. Pulling it open, he stepped outside for a couple of moments, and she heard him murmur something to someone outside.

Then he returned, shutting the door behind him.

'I was just going to say that I don't want anything,' she said.

'You're assuming the refreshments are for you.' He strolled closer, loose and easy as a panther on the prowl. 'Perhaps they're for me. Perhaps I need some liquid courage in order to ask you to be my wife.'

A man less in need of liquid courage she couldn't imagine.

Her fingers curled into fists at her sides as he came even closer, stalking her, and her heartbeat was rocketing around in her chest like a bird desperate to find its way out of its cage. She was afraid. Of him and what he could unleash in her. What he'd *already* unleashed in her. If he got any closer...

Stop. You're letting your emotions do your thinking for you. Again.

Willow gritted her teeth and ignored her frantic heartbeat, shoved away her fear. She was cool, collected and in control. She was *not* the girl who'd hurt her father. She was the woman who would fix him.

'Your Grace...' she began, pleased with how uninflected her voice was.

'Oh, no, not "Your Grace".' Mercifully he stopped a couple of paces away from her. 'My father liked an honorific, but I'm not one for formality.' His smile reminded her of a very wicked, very hungry wolf. 'As you've probably noticed by now.'

His shirt was open at the neck, exposing the strong,

tanned column of his throat, and found herself wondering what his skin would taste like if she kissed him there. And what he would do if she did…

'I don't care what you'd prefer to be called,' she said. 'I'd prefer not to call you anything at all. Just say what you have to say and then I can go home.'

He stared at her a moment longer, like a predator deciding whether or not to pounce, and her pulse started to climb, excitement and a strange, fearful anticipation winding tightly around her.

But just then a knock came on the door, mercifully catching the Duke's attention, and as he turned and moved to open it Willow felt as if she'd earned a reprieve of some kind.

A member of staff came in carrying a tray in one hand and a bottle in the other. He deposited the tray on the coffee table by the couch, put the bottle beside it, then left. The tray contained a selection of cheeses and crackers, two long-stemmed glasses, and a steaming cup of tea.

The Duke moved over to the tray and picked up the tea. 'There is champagne, of course, but I thought you might prefer something a little more calming.' He carried it over to the small table that stood next to the armchair closest to the fireplace and set it down. 'Please. Sit.'

She didn't want to sit. And she didn't want tea. What she wanted was to walk out of the door and flee back to the safety of her home, or anywhere really as long it was away from his disturbing presence. But that would be to admit he affected her, and, since he'd already overwhelmed her control twice already, she decided there would not be a third time.

She was stronger than that.

So she moved over to the armchair and sat down, pointedly ignoring the tea.

He gave her an amused look, as if he'd expected exactly that, then sat down in the armchair opposite, long legs stretched out in front of him.

'So,' he said. 'My proposal. Thornhaven, as you know, is my family estate and, as I'm the only child, it should automatically come to me following my father's death. However, a couple of codicils in his will have come to light and it has become apparent that I can only inherit after two stipulations have been fulfilled. The first being that I must be married.'

Willow studied him. He didn't seem all that cut up about his father's quite recent death, which was puzzling. Perhaps they hadn't got on. 'That seems very…'

'Old-fashioned?' the Duke finished. 'Yes. Remarkably so. My father was a very old-fashioned kind of man, not to mention vindictive. But that's another story.'

It certainly sounded like a story. But not one she was interested in, sadly for him.

'What has this got to do with me marrying you?'

'My personal assistant found a note in my father's papers signed by your father, promising a marriage between the Seventh Duke of Audley and your father's eldest and yet unborn daughter.' He gave her that predator's smile again. 'I am the Seventh Duke of Audley and you, I believe, are your father's eldest daughter.'

Willow smoothed her already smooth jeans then clasped her fidgeting hands in her lap. 'Yes, but my father said it was a gentleman's agreement. A hand-shake that they both then forgot about.'

'He certainly forgot about the note, yet that is indeed in existence.'

'You think I'm going to agree to marry you because of some note?'

'Of course not.' Blue gleamed from beneath thick black lashes. 'I'm not a fool, Diana.'

Heat rose in her face. She was letting him get to her again, wasn't she?

Glancing away, she found herself staring at the cup full of tea. She could smell its faint, slightly citrusy scent. It looked to be her favourite kind too, Earl Grey with a slice of lemon. 'I'm not sure why you think I'm going to marry you based entirely on some long-forgotten agreement your father had with mine. It's nonsense.'

His laugh was soft and deep and sexy, and she remembered that too. He'd laughed down by the lake and she'd been shocked by it, since she'd never heard such a warm sound. It shocked and transfixed her now.

'You're right,' he said, as if he had no idea the effect his amusement had on her. 'It is nonsense. But I can make it nonsense that is very much worth your while.'

'And how are you going to do that?'

The gleam in his eyes intensified. 'With money, of course.'

'You mean you'll pay me to marry you?'

'Exactly. It's not a love match, obviously. I prefer

to think of it as a business arrangement. You allow me to marry you and I pay you for the privilege of having your name on the marriage certificate.'

Loath as she was to admit it, there was a certain cool logic to the idea. And the calm, dispassionate way he talked about it, calling it a 'business arrangement', helped too.

Perhaps there was merit in it. Her father would at last be able to get the help he needed and she would finally be able to go to university.

She met his gaze. 'How much are we talking about here?'

'I take it you're interested?'

'In the money, certainly.' A sudden suspicion gripped her. 'But you knew that, didn't you?'

He didn't even blink. 'Yes, I knew that. *I* did my research.'

She could feel herself flush again, but ignored it. 'Give me a figure.'

He leaned back in his chair in a lazy movement. Giving every impression of being at his leisure, and yet his eyes gleamed hot. 'How much? How does this sound?' And he named a price that stole her breath entirely away.

It was a lot of money. A *lot* of money. Enough for the expensive treatments her father had wanted. Enough for an entirely new house that would enable him to live more independently than he was doing now. And definitely more than enough for her live comfortably while she studied.

'You're joking.' Her voice was breathless with shock.

He didn't seem at all bothered. 'Oh, I assure you I'm not.'

'But that kind of money? Purely to get married?'

'Yes, well, you remember I said that there were two stipulations?'

Willow's gut lurched. 'And what is the other?'

He gazed at her steadily from beneath his lashes, that wicked smile playing around his beautiful mouth. 'I must also have a son.'

Her eyes went wide, her mouth opening slightly.

Poor Diana. This was not at all what she'd been expecting, was it?

Achilles didn't move, keeping his posture relaxed. He would have to go carefully here, because yes, this would be shocking to her. And her instinct would be to refuse. Which meant he'd have to walk a very thin line.

She'd already revealed herself to be passionate and that she had a temper. And he could see, too, a certain stubbornness in the firm line of her jaw and the tilt of her chin. A woman who did not like being told what to do. And really, why should she?

If his research was correct, she'd spent the last nine years caring and providing for her father, which meant that, although she might be relatively young, she had a certain maturity. He could not simply fling some money at her and expect her to fall at his feet. Nor, he suspected, would simple charm work. At least, not to tempt her into motherhood.

He would need a more complex plan.

'So let me get this straight,' she said at last, her voice flat. 'Not only do you want me to marry you, but you want me to have your child too.'

'Yes.'

'That's…madness.'

Achilles spread his hands. 'What can I say? When I told you my father was old-fashioned, I meant it.'

'Why?' She was sitting bolt upright in the armchair, the tea he'd brought her untouched. He hadn't really expected her to drink it, but he had seen her glance longingly at it, and he filed the information away for future reference. 'Why on earth would he make those stipulations?'

'Because he's a vindictive old bastard? Who knows? But I assure you I went over that will with a fine-toothed comb. There are no loopholes.' He could tell her about Ulysses now, but what would be the point? She didn't need to know.

She put her hands on the arm of the chair. 'You can't be serious.'

'Oh, but I am. Deadly serious.' He tilted his head, watching her. 'However, I agree it's a big ask. Hence the amount of money I'm willing to pay in recompense.'

'You can't possibly think I'll agree to it.'

'Actually, people agree to the strangest things when money is involved.' He gave her another smile, non-threatening and pleasant. 'But I can see you're not convinced. Well, that's fine. I thought it wouldn't hurt to try.' Pushing himself out of the armchair, he rose to his feet. 'Don't fret, Diana. I have other options.'

She blinked, clearly surprised. 'So…that's it?'

'What did you expect? That I would march you at gunpoint to the altar? Of course not. That would be far too mediaeval of me. Well, don't let me keep you.' Achilles turned and strolled casually to the door, pulling it open. 'You probably have a lot to do and I don't want to take up any more of your valuable time.'

He'd unbalanced her, that was clear. Which was all part of his plan. If she didn't like being told what to do, he wouldn't tell her. He would coax her into it, seduce her. She was probably wise to a bit of reverse psychology, but he guessed that she wouldn't be able to help questioning him all the same. She needed that money and desperately.

Sure enough, she said, 'But I thought you needed a wife?'

'And I do. Not to mention a son. But as I said, I have a number of other options.' He raised a brow. 'Did you think you were the only one I was considering?'

Her lovely mouth opened, then shut, a certain amount of bewilderment flickering over her face. 'If you have other options, then why ask me?'

'I told you. The agreement between our fathers. I thought it was polite to ask you first.'

'Polite,' she echoed, as if she didn't understand the word.

'Yes.' He nodded towards the door. 'Please, don't stay any longer than you need to on my account.'

But she was now looking at him fixedly and he

felt the kick of satisfaction deep inside. The hook was baited and she'd had a taste of it. All he had to do was reel her in, but again, he'd need to be careful. It wouldn't do to rush this.

'So what exactly are you expecting from a marriage?' she asked. 'Apart from a child?'

He let none of his satisfaction show. Now was the time to lay out what he wanted and there was no point holding back or making it seem less than it was. There was a time for honesty in business and there was a time for subterfuge, and now was the time for honesty.

He didn't want anything to come back to bite him when she finally agreed, because she would agree. Of that he had no doubt.

'If you're thinking it would be marriage in name only then you would be wrong.' He looked straight at her, let her see that he was giving her the pure, unvarnished truth. 'Considering our chemistry, I would very much like to conceive a child naturally. However, until that happens, our lives will remain separate. There is no need for you to live with me, for example. And once the child is born, we can get an amicable divorce and you can go on your way. You'll have access to the child, if you wish, but it will stay with me.' Now was the time to add the sweetener. 'If you agree, I will pay you the amount of money I specified, plus see to any other needs you may have. Your father may continue to live in his home with a caregiver, though I hear there are some excellent treatment facilities in the south of France, which I would be happy to pay for. Certainly the weather there is better.'

At first, he'd considered a marriage in name only and the conception of the child via medical assistance. His father's will hadn't stipulated any other requirements such as living together or being a proper family. He would of course raise the child himself, since there was no way he'd risk the chance of any child of his having the kind of upbringing he'd had.

But all those initial ideas had changed over the course of this meeting, coalescing into a single, bright, shining whole.

He would have her. And why not? He wanted her and she wanted him, which meant the sex would be phenomenal. And it would make conception extremely pleasurable into the bargain. And once that was accomplished, they could go their separate ways. Of course, a child needed their mother—his own mother had left when he was ten and so he knew how that felt—and he wouldn't deny her access if she wanted it.

But it wouldn't be a permanent arrangement between them, not when he had no idea what kind of mother Willow would be. And after his own experiences, the last thing he wanted was to expose a child to a parent who didn't care.

People said that love was infinite, but people were liars. Love had a shelf life. It was limited. And when it ran out, there was no more to be had. Certainly his parents' supply had been exhausted by the time he was born and Willow's could very well be the same.

Regardless, he couldn't risk it, which meant the child would remain with him. Of course, his own heart had been burned out long ago, but he could pretend.

He'd certainly make damn sure the child never felt the lack of care and attention. No child of his would ever feel like a ghost.

Yes, it all made perfect sense to him and he would get what he wanted in the end.

He always did.

She blinked and he could see her mind working, going over the possibilities of what he'd said.

He smiled. 'Well, I can see you're not interested, that's clear.'

Her gaze abruptly focused on him. 'You think anyone will be?'

'Oh, I know of many women who will be.' He allowed just a hint of heat into his eyes. 'Like I said, I have many options when it comes to choosing a wife. And some of them wouldn't even require any financial recompense. In fact, for some, just having access to my bed would be more than enough.'

Willow made a sceptical sound, but he could see the blush that tinged her cheeks. She was already imagining herself in his bed, he'd lay money on it.

'However, it's not for you, I can see that,' he murmured, because now that he'd piqued her interest it was time to send her on her way to think about it. 'Your father must be waiting for you. Please don't allow me to keep you.'

She stared at him for a long moment, her eyes narrowing. Some part of her might be aware that he was playing her, but, since he wasn't forcing her into anything, she wouldn't be able to tell how.

But he couldn't force this anyway. It would have to be her choice.

And if she doesn't choose you?

She would choose him. It was inevitable. He'd weighted the dice and they would fall in his favour.

He would make sure of it.

After a second's hesitation, Willow pushed herself out of the armchair and walked hesitantly to the door of the room. He didn't take his eyes off her, watching her the whole way, allowing some of the heat their chemistry generated to flood the space between them in case she needed a reminder that it wasn't only money he could give her.

She paused beside him, no sign of a flush in her cheeks now. Her eyes had lost that smoky, molten look, glittering like hard little jewels. She'd cooled, a volcano gone dormant.

'I'm sorry,' she said, not sounding sorry in the least. 'But I can't give you what you want.'

'I understand. Like I said, I have plenty of options.' He held out his hand to her. 'Thank you for coming.'

After a moment's hesitation, she gave it to him, which was a mistake she'd surely kick herself for later. Because he took it in his and turned it over, laying a kiss in the middle of her palm.

Her breath caught, sparks flickering in her eyes.

So, the volcano wasn't quite as dormant as he thought.

He was tempted to lengthen the moment, intensify it. But everything was so finely balanced that he didn't want to push, and already the kiss might have been a step too far.

So he let go of her hand before she'd even opened her mouth to protest. 'Goodbye, Diana,' he said, and stepped back.

She looked as if she wanted to say something, but then, clearly thinking better of it, she only murmured, 'Goodbye,' and went out.

Achilles closed the door behind her.

And smiled.

CHAPTER FOUR

WILLOW STOOD IN front of the dusty fireplace in the living room, unclasping then re-clasping her hands, trying to stay calm. She hadn't thought this would be so hard, and yet with her father sitting there in his usual chair, the tea she'd made him sitting on the table beside him untouched, that disapproving, cold stare on his face, she found it was more difficult than she'd expected.

She'd just finished telling him about her meeting with the Duke the night before, and what the offer had been. And then how she'd flatly refused, because she'd had to. Of course she had to. Because it wasn't a 'business arrangement' after all. No, the Duke wanted them to conceive his child naturally, and she couldn't do that. She just…couldn't.

Especially not after reading everything that had turned up in the internet search she'd done the night before as soon as she'd got home.

Achilles 'Temple' Templeton, the Seventh Duke of Audley, appeared to be one of the most notorious playboys in Europe, if not the entire world, and had the reputation to prove it. Which, remembering him from the night before, did not surprise her.

That he was also the head of a worldwide, high-risk venture-capital firm did. She knew next to nothing about playboys, but had always assumed that they cared more about parties than they did about business, though it seemed that the Duke of Audley was an exception.

Then again, given his behaviour the night before and what she knew about him now, that shouldn't be a surprise either. He was clearly a man used to negotiation, used to driving a hard bargain, and being utterly ruthless about it. He was certainly a man used to getting his own way.

He'd used those business tactics on her and she'd been well aware of it at the time. Letting her know that she was his first choice, and yet being clear that he had other options. Before putting her off-balance by ending the meeting before she was ready.

A little reverse psychology, of course. If she'd been thinking straight, she would have given him a dose of his own medicine. But she hadn't been thinking straight. She'd been shocked and angry and overwhelmed, and he'd taken advantage of that shamelessly.

It made her want to refuse him out of sheer principle.

But that her father would never understand. She hoped he'd understand her caveats about the 'natural conception' proposal, but, judging from the way he was looking at her, it was clear he didn't understand that either.

'What exactly is the nature of the problem, Willow?' he asked coldly. 'Is it the…physical interaction?'

Heat burned in her cheeks. She didn't want to be having this discussion with her father, but there was no help for it. He'd been in bed by the time she'd got home the night before, which had given her a brief reprieve, but this morning the first thing he'd wanted to know was how it had gone. And now, why she'd refused.

'Dad, please,' she said repressively. 'Do I really need to go into detail?'

But her father's sharp, dark stare was unavoidable. 'You're assigning emotion to what is essentially a bodily function, Willow. There's no need for embarrassment, just as there's no need to make a fuss about it. It's also no reason to refuse his very generous offer.'

Her heart was beating very fast and her palms were sweaty, and she felt the almost impossible-to-ignore urge to move, to pace up and down, get this agitation out somehow. It reminded her of being a little girl again, full of that insatiable, hungry energy that made it very difficult for her to sit still. That little girl who felt everything so deeply—too deeply. The little girl whose demands used to annoy her father so much he would lock her out of the house for the entire day.

No wonder he was looking at her with such disapproval.

Willow's jaw ached with the effort it took to force away her agitation, to stiffen herself into rigidity so she wouldn't fidget.

It was the Duke's fault, of course. All of this was *his* fault. If he hadn't been the man who'd kissed her beside the lake, the man who'd made her lose her temper and nearly slap him, and who'd kissed her a second time in front of the fireplace in Thornhaven…

If he hadn't been that man, then none of this would have been a problem.

She would have accepted his proposal without if not a second thought, then at least a third thought.

But he was that man and so she couldn't risk it.

It's not him that's the issue. It's you.

Her jaw got even tighter and she was conscious of her father's gaze on her, cold and disapproving. How could she explain to him what the issue was? That she was afraid of being in the Duke's presence because twice now he'd made her forget herself? That even the touch of his hand and a glance from his relentless blue gaze made her feel shaky with anger and desperate with a hunger she didn't understand?

Yes, it was true. It wasn't the Duke himself she was afraid of but of his effect on her. Her reminded her of how she had used to be, wild and uncontained and at the mercy of her own emotions. Of how demanding and difficult she'd been, a howling whirlwind of rage that had culminated in the tantrum that had led to her father collapsing on the floor at her feet as the stroke had taken him.

She didn't want to be that girl again.

'It's not that simple, Dad,' she said flatly, not wanting to go into it.

'Yes, it is,' her father disagreed. 'Be logical for once in your life. The money will enable me to be more independent and you to do whatever you want to do. I don't understand why you're even hesitating.'

No, he didn't understand, as she'd suspected he wouldn't. For her father logic was everything, while emotions were suspect and weren't to be trusted. And he had reason, she knew that. He'd loved her mother passionately and had been devastated by her death, and the only way to ease the pain had been to cut it entirely out of his heart.

So he had.

But he was right, though. Refusing the money that would give them a much better quality of life simply because she was scared of how the Duke made her feel was utterly ridiculous. Her emotional responses were always suspect, so why was she even taking any notice of them?

She let out a breath, rubbed her palms down her jeans, ignoring the old urge to run into the woods the way she had used to as a child.

'He wants a son, Dad,' she said. 'You did hear that, didn't you?'

Clarence shrugged. 'Then give him one. He'd look after it, you said? If so, then that shouldn't be a problem. It's nothing that people haven't done before. And it's probably better to do it sooner rather than later, when you have a career.'

The offhand way he said it stabbed at something deep inside her. He hadn't wanted her, and he'd told her that on more than one occasion. He'd only agreed to have her because her mother had wanted a baby and he'd loved her mother, not out of any desire for a child himself.

And this would be the same, wouldn't it? She hadn't

wanted children, not after her own experience of growing up, and certainly the emotional commitment it took
to be a parent wasn't something she could do.

Then again, the Duke had said that the child would
stay with him. She wouldn't have to be involved in the
process of bringing it up.

History would repeat itself.

A lump rose in her throat. She stared down at the
threadbare carpet and forced it away. No, it wouldn't
be history repeating itself. It wouldn't be having a child
she didn't want for someone else, condemning them
to be brought up by a mother who hadn't wanted them
in the first place.

The Duke had said he would keep the child and she
would have access to it, if she wanted. He was rich.
The child would live in luxury and have every opportunity. And he'd no doubt be a much more stable and
steady parent than she would ever be. She was, after
all, quite volatile and impatient, both of which weren't
great traits for a mother.

But would he be able to give a child love?

Good question. The Duke wasn't exactly a family
man by all accounts. And yet what was the alternative?
If she didn't marry the Duke, her father would be stuck
here in this half-life, where he couldn't do the things he
wanted because the house couldn't accommodate him.
Because she was too physically weak to provide him
with the support he needed. And there was the constant struggle for money and all the bills that needed
paying that her wages from the cafe barely covered…

If you don't do this, he'll blame you even more than he already does.

The lump in her throat became larger. She'd ruined his life; how could she ruin it any more?

'What if I...want to be in the child's life?' she asked, even though she hadn't meant to.

Her father lifted a shaking hand. Once those hands had been rock steady, able to cut and stitch even the smallest arteries. Now he could barely manage to lift his teacup. 'You won't,' he said tersely. 'Children are hard work.' His hand must have been shaking harder than normal, because although he managed to get it to his mouth for a sip, when he put it back down it clipped the side of the saucer and fell over, spilling hot tea everywhere.

Instantly Willow dashed to the kitchen, grabbing a cloth to mop it up, her father sitting there in stony silence.

His was a cold anger, diamond hard and bright, full of sharp edges that sometimes felt like knives against her skin. She could feel those knives now, cutting into her, leaving her in no doubt as to who he blamed for the spill. Not his shaking hand, but her.

She was the reason he'd lost his career and his health, his independence.

Her and her anger.

You can't refuse the Duke. Not if it means leaving your father like this.

No, it was true. They needed the money too urgently. Her father needed better care and, since she was the reason he was sitting in this chair, his career—his whole life—in ruins, then it made only logical sense for her to be the one to fix it.

But she wasn't going to give the Duke everything. She had to draw the line somewhere to protect herself too.

She would marry him, but she wouldn't sleep with him. And she'd give him the child he wanted, but only via medical assistance. Her father would find her reasoning flawed, but then, her father wasn't the one who had to do this. She did. And she could tell herself all she liked that the Duke didn't affect her, that she was stronger than the chemistry that leapt between them, but twice was enough to tell her what lies those were.

Better to be intelligent about it and nip temptation in the bud before it had a chance to grow.

The Duke would no doubt argue, since he was clearly a man used to getting his own way, but he could find other women for his bed. He didn't need her.

Willow gave her father a last mop up with the cloth and then went back into the kitchen, dumping it in the sink before coming back out again.

'You're right,' she said flatly. 'I'll do it. I'll marry him.'

Her father's expression lost a little of that hard, cold edge. 'I knew you'd come to your senses eventually.' He nodded approvingly. 'Good girl.'

She ignored the little glow in her chest his good opinion always gave her. Cut it away.

She was doing this for duty's sake, nothing more.

Achilles gave her two days. If she hadn't come back to him after that, then he'd have to reassess his plan, but she'd come back to him, he was certain.

The money would make an attractive package, and, though she'd balked at the idea of sleeping with him, he'd seen the hunger in her eyes. Had tasted it too in her kiss. She was passionate and she wanted him, and if she agreed to his plan he would make sure she wouldn't regret it.

He thought about staying in Yorkshire until she'd made a decision, but he hated being at Thornhaven and, since he never waited on someone else's pleasure, he took a helicopter down to London for a few days, giving his staff strict instructions that, should Willow Hall make contact, he was to be told immediately.

He was in the top-floor meeting room of his building in the City, in the middle of a discussion with some top execs from an Italian tech company, when Jane knocked on the door then put her head around it.

Achilles didn't like to be disturbed or interrupted while he was conducting business, but Jane never did so if it wasn't urgent, so all he did was raise an enquiring eyebrow.

'Sorry to interrupt,' she said briskly, 'but I thought you'd want to know that I have Willow Hall on the line.'

A pulse of the most intense electricity went through him, deep satisfaction following behind it.

Of course she would come back to him. There had never been any doubt.

'Thank you, Jane,' he said calmly, allowing none of that satisfaction to show on his face. Then he looked back at the execs sitting around the meeting-room table. 'Ladies and gentlemen, I'm afraid I have an urgent matter to attend to. I'm sure you won't mind if we adjourn this till tomorrow.'

Naturally, nobody minded. Or if they did, they didn't dare say.

He got Jane to put Willow through to his mobile phone immediately, then turned his chair to face the window, looking out over London shimmering in the summer heat. He waited a moment then said, 'Miss Hall? This is a surprise.'

There was a slight pause.

'Is it?' Her voice, sweet and husky, held a hint of asperity.

'Of course.' He leaned back in his chair. 'You were very clear that you wanted no part of my offer.'

'Yes, about that...' She sounded very cool and yet he could hear the uncertainty beneath it. 'I've had a chance to think about what you offered me a couple of days ago, and on reflection... Well, I might have been a bit too hasty in refusing.'

'I see.' He let no hint of triumph colour his voice. 'Have you had a change of heart, then?'

'Possibly. If your offer is still open, of course.'

He rested one foot on the opposite knee, gazing at the light glittering off the windows of the city below him. 'I have been pursuing other options, as I mentioned in our interview,' he lied smoothly, because it wouldn't do to let her know he'd been doing nothing but waiting for her. 'But I haven't settled on anyone yet, if that's what you're asking.'

'Oh.' Another slight pause before she went on. 'In

that case you should know that I've changed my mind. I would like to accept your offer.'

Satisfaction twisted hard in his chest, his smile reflected back from the windows in front of him sharp and white as a tiger's.

So, he would have it. His brother's inheritance. His brother's title and his house, and his wife. Except it wouldn't be his brother's any longer.

It would be his.

Idly, he wondered whether his father was spinning in his grave yet.

'There is just one condition,' Willow said.

For a second, too lost in his own triumph, Achilles didn't hear her.

Then he did.

He frowned. 'A condition?'

'Yes.' Now she was very cool and collected, no trace of uncertainty. 'It's just a small thing.'

Achilles was not in the habit of granting conditions. However, he wasn't an unreasonable man and he knew what he was asking from her was a lot.

'And what thing would that be?' he asked, keeping the question casual.

'That the marriage will be in name only.' Her voice was firm, unwavering. 'And that the child should be conceived with medical assistance.'

Achilles went very still. 'That was not the offer I made.'

'I realise that. However, you did say it was a business arrangement. In which case you should consider this a counter-offer.'

He stared at his own reflection in the windows opposite him, the tiger's smile vanishing, the intensity of his disappointment surprising him.

Did you really expect her to agree to everything?

Yes. Yes, he had. She was passionate and she wanted him, that had been obvious to him the moment he'd first spotted her watching him swimming in the lake.

He didn't think he'd been wrong. He knew when a woman desired him. She'd certainly kissed him as if she was dying for him, and he was certain it hadn't been an act. So what was the problem?

Good question. One you could ask yourself.

Denial had never bothered him before, not that it happened very often, but still. So her refusal shouldn't be an issue. And yet it was. And he had a sneaking suspicion he knew why. That it was about how she'd made him feel out there beside the lake and in the sitting room of Thornhaven, the fire of her passion lighting him up, chasing away the ghosts of his past. Making him feel alive.

And which in turn made him uneasy. He didn't like acceding her any power and yet there was no denying that she had some. Otherwise why would he be feeling so annoyed about it?

'Can I ask why?' He made sure he sounded as calm and as cool as she did. That he was not disappointed in any way. 'You seemed to enjoy the kisses we shared. Or did I overstep?'

'No,' she said quietly. 'You didn't overstep. And yes, I...enjoyed them. But you're a stranger to me. And I'm afraid I don't know you well enough to sleep with you.'

'You don't have to know anyone well in order to sleep with them, Diana,' he said before he could stop himself. 'In fact, sometimes it's better if you don't.'

'That might be the way you do things, but it's not the way I do them. I don't sleep with people I don't know.'

Annoyance sank claws into him, but he fought it down, because that wasn't going to help. No, it wasn't about her or what she gave him, it was about what she represented.

If he didn't claim her as his wife in the most basic way, then she could hardly be his, could she? Then again, in order for her to be his, he only needed to have one night with her. They didn't have to keep sleeping together.

He stayed silent a moment, turning the thought over in his head.

She was clearly a woman who knew her own mind and would not be pushed. In which case he wouldn't push.

'Very well,' he said coolly. 'So, how did you imagine this business arrangement would progress?'

'Obviously to where we'd lead separate lives. I'll live at the cottage and you can live…wherever you like.' She paused briefly. 'I won't expect you to be faithful. As long as you're discreet, I'm sure it won't be a problem for you to take lovers.'

Part of him was outraged that she'd somehow managed to take control and start offering conditions as if the whole thing had been her idea, while another part of him was amused and not a little admiring of her audacity, not to mention her intelligence.

'Discreet?' he couldn't help saying. 'You did do your research about me, didn't you?'

'Yes, I'm aware of your reputation. But I'm sure that will change once you have a family to consider.'

He nearly laughed at her cool certainty that he'd do exactly what she asked, despite the fact that it was something he'd already decided to do himself.

'Of course,' he murmured. 'And I'm sure you will do the same when it comes to lovers.'

'I will not be having lovers,' she said crisply. 'I'll be too busy attending university. But, as I said, if you want them then I won't mind.'

University, hmm? Interesting.

'That's very gracious of you,' he drawled. 'But somehow I fail to see how a woman as passionate as yourself can go years without having sex at least once. Or are you planning on taking your vows?'

'That's really none of your business. But I've managed very well so far and I don't see that changing any time soon.'

Surprise rippled through him, though, on reflection, it shouldn't. 'You're a virgin?'

'Well… I… I mean… I don't think…' She stopped, sounding flustered. 'So? What if I am? It doesn't matter anyway.'

It shouldn't matter. He preferred not to deal with virgins. He preferred women who knew what they were doing.

Yet somehow it did matter.

She will be completely yours.

That thought made the blood pump hard in his veins,

a primitive, almost Neanderthal reaction. But it was true. She would be his in a way that Thornhaven would never be. That the title would never be. Because they were all things that Ulysses had once had.

But Ulysses had never had her.

Achilles didn't think. The idea was already in his head and so he said, 'In that case, I have a condition to your condition.'

There was a small silence.

'Oh?' She sounded wary now. 'What condition?'

The tiger's smile was back, the reflection in the mirror looking hungry. He wanted this and he would have it. He was *owed*. For all the years of neglect. For all the years of feeling as if he was the ghost, not his brother. For all the years of anguish, trying so very hard to be the boy his parents had lost so they would love him too.

Never realising that they had had no love left to give him.

'I want a wedding night,' he said in a voice that didn't sound like his. That wasn't either lazy or seductive. That was stripped to bare bones.

'Excuse me?'

She didn't sound quite so cool now and that was just as well. Time she learned that this was his show, not hers.

'I think you heard me.' He swung the chair gently back and forth on its pivot. 'I am happy for you to have a separate life and do whatever you choose. Go to university, see whomever you want, or not, as the case may be. But I want a wedding night.'

'Why?' Her voice was sharp. 'If it's just sex you want you can get that from any woman.'

It was true, he could. But it wasn't just sex that he wanted.

It was sex with her. With the woman who should have been his brother's.

'But it's not just sex that I want, Diana.' He couldn't give her the whole story, but he could give her some of it. It would admit her some power, yet he knew, as he had back at Thornhaven, that now was the time for honesty. And that he wouldn't get what he wanted unless he gave it to her. 'I want sex with *you*.'

'Me?' This time she sounded shocked. 'But... I... why should that matter?'

'You have passion. And I am a connoisseur of passion. I want yours and I think that perhaps you want mine too.'

She said nothing.

And suddenly he found himself on the edge of his seat, tension gripping him, every part of him focused on the phone in his hand and on the woman on the other end of the line.

'One night,' he said in that bare-bones voice, all his seductive techniques deserting him, leaving only demand left. 'That's all I will ever ask of you. Just one. And I can tell you this with absolute confidence, that if you want to enjoy your first time with a man then I am the man you should enjoy it with.'

More silence.

'That's the most arrogant thing I've ever heard anyone say,' she said at last.

He wanted to smile, but not because he was amused. 'I have never pretended to be anything other than what I am. And yes, I can be arrogant at times. But if you know my reputation then you will also know that women do not go away from my bed unsatisfied.' He felt himself wound tight as a spring. 'I will make it a night to remember, I promise you.'

Yet more silence, longer this time.

You sound as if you're begging. Since when did you ever beg?

He didn't like that thought. Didn't like that thought at all. It made him feel the way he had with his father, constantly hoping that one day it would happen. That his father would see the son he had right in front of him instead of being obsessed with the one he had lost.

Theos, why had he said anything? Why had he granted her even this modicum of power over him?

Too late to regret it now.

'Just one night?' she said at last. 'One night and that's all?'

He didn't move. 'Yes. One night and that's all.'

The silence this time felt like the longest stretch of time he'd ever experienced.

'All right.' Her voice was breathless. 'You can have a wedding night.'

Then she disconnected the call.

CHAPTER FIVE

THE DUKE MOVED with unsurprising efficiency.

The next day a courier arrived on Willow's doorstep with a thick-looking folder of legal documents that proved to be a contract cementing her agreement to marriage and a child legally. Which stood to reason. This was a business agreement after all.

So she sat down and spent the entire day combing through it, making sure she understood everything. It was clear and unequivocal and there were no loopholes of any kind. The Duke's ruthless business reputation was obviously well earned.

You'll soon find out if his other reputation was also well earned.

The thought wound through her head, the words of the contract blurring in front of her as the memory of the previous night's conversation abruptly hit.

'I want a wedding night.'

Willow's heartbeat sped up, the throb of some deep and inexplicable ache gathering inside her.

She still wasn't sure quite why she'd agreed to a wedding night when she'd been so sure that she wasn't going to sleep with him. Or how she'd somehow let slip that she was a virgin.

The latter, because she'd wanted to shock him maybe. But the former…

He'd told her he wanted her passion, and after that his voice had gone deeper, rough, no longer quite so lazy or seductive. Almost as if he was desperate, which a part of her had liked far too much.

She, the little virgin from Yorkshire, had the world's most notorious playboy begging her for a wedding night.

She'd said yes before she'd thought twice about it.

He wanted her. And more than that, he wanted her passion, and no one had wanted that in so very long. She also couldn't deny that she wanted him in return.

It was probably a mistake, probably a sign of her general lack of control, but surely one night wouldn't hurt? Just one. Her wedding night. And after all, he'd basically insisted. She really couldn't say no, could she?

Dismissing the thoughts of the wedding night, Willow read on, the terms for the child giving her another lurch of doubt. It was strange seeing it in black and white, her agreement to provide him with a son. A big undertaking, especially when she'd never thought about having children herself. And most especially considering the child would live with the Duke and not with her.

Yet, as she'd thought earlier, that would be the best thing for the child. She wasn't motherhood material after all. She could visit though, the Duke had promised her that, and she would. A child should know its mother, even if that mother wasn't a particularly good one.

That all of these were rationalisations she knew deep in her heart, but she decided it was better not to think about them too deeply. The most important thing was that she and her father got the money that the Duke promised them.

Sure enough, after she'd signed the contract and sent it away, the money landed in her bank account. Then a car and a nurse arrived to take her father to a renowned stroke specialist for an assessment and some recommendations for further treatments at her father's preferred facility in the south of France. It was horrifically expensive, but the Duke agreed to cover the cost without hesitation and soon arranged for her father to travel there after the wedding.

Willow had expected some registry-office ceremony, conducted swiftly and without much fanfare, since it wasn't as if they were making vows of love in front of friends and family. But apparently that was not what the Duke wanted.

A small ceremony with a 'few hundred' of his closest friends was what the Duke wanted, though she wasn't sure why he seemed so set on making a big deal out of it.

He also wanted to discuss it with her, suggesting she join him in London at her earliest convenience. She didn't particularly want to discuss it with him, since she didn't much care about the wedding itself, but, as refusing to go just because she found his presence threatening would be admitting far too much, and her father now had a full-time caregiver, she felt she had no choice but to agree.

And so a few days later she found herself on a helicopter flying south, a building nervousness along with a strange sense of anticipation collecting inside of her.

She tried to ignore both sensations by watching the unrolling green of the countryside below her and attempting to enjoy the novelty of flying, since she'd never been in any kind of aircraft before, let alone a helicopter.

But all too soon they were approaching London and once again she was faced with the reality of having to be in the Duke's disturbing, compelling and dangerous presence. The thought made her heart beat fast and her palms feel sweaty.

The helicopter circled around the City of London before zeroing in on a particular building. The Duke had told her that he'd fly her directly to his office where they could chat in peace and this was clearly it.

Willow gripped tightly to her usual distance as the helicopter came in to land on the building's rooftop helipad, and when she got out she was instantly surrounded by people.

A no-nonsense, businesslike woman who introduced herself as Jane, Temple's PA, whisked her down to the waiting room outside the Duke's office.

It was the most luxurious waiting room Willow had ever seen, with thick, pale, silvery carpet and black leather furniture. Black and white abstract photographs on the walls. Clean and minimalist and looking extraordinarily expensive.

Willow's heart began to beat even faster and she had to resist wiping her palms down on the light summer dress she wore. When she'd put it on in her bedroom earlier she hadn't given it much thought, since she wasn't used to fussing around with her appearance. It had been cool, and that was the extent of her thinking.

Now, in amongst all this sophistication and quiet luxury, about to meet the man who unbalanced her so completely, she felt underdressed and shabby, as though she'd gone to a ball in her nightgown by mistake.

It made her temper shift, the veneer of her thin control cracking, and she had to grit her teeth hard to hold on to it and not let it escape. Because bad things happened when she lost her temper. Very bad things.

Jane led her to the big double doors of the Duke's office and then pushed them open, ushering her inside.

The Duke himself was standing by the floor-to-ceiling windows that looked out over the city. It was the most magnificent view, though it wasn't the view that immediately drew the eye. How could a mere view compete with the man who stood there as if he owned it?

Dressed in a dark charcoal suit that highlighted the width of his powerful shoulders and lean waist, he was a commanding, magnetic presence as he talked on the phone to someone. That deep, rich, melted-chocolate voice filled the room, whispering over her skin and making her shiver. He wasn't speaking English but some language she didn't recognise—Greek maybe?—and the musical sound of it was a delight that held her unexpectedly mesmerised.

She wasn't aware of when Jane backed out silently. She didn't notice the doors shutting behind her. She even forgot about her temper.

All she was aware of was the man by the windows, the taut electricity of his presence surrounding her and stealing all her breath.

Who are you kidding? You couldn't resist a wedding night and you know it. And now you don't have to.

Something inside her gave a strange little twist and then relaxed, as if she'd had her hair in an overly tight bun the whole day and then had let it down.

Perhaps it was being away from the cottage and Yorkshire, away from her father, that was affecting her, because all of a sudden a loose, easy feeling flooded through her, the tension in her muscles gradually unwinding.

She'd agreed to marry him. She'd signed a legally binding contract and there was no escaping it. She'd also agreed to a wedding night, one that he'd argued for, because he'd wanted her. And not just her; he wanted her passion too.

So what was the point in resisting him? What was the point in controlling herself?

Perhaps you should give him a taste of who you really are...

Willow took a silent, shaken breath as the idea took hold, a combination of excitement and trepidation gripping her. And why not? He'd wanted that passion, had told her he couldn't get it from anyone else, and so really she was duty bound to give it to him. Of course, once he found out who she truly was, he'd probably realise, as her father had, that she was too much trouble to bother with. Not that she cared.

She had her university plans and no doubt they'd soon be starting the procedure for having a child. His opinion of her was the least of her worries.

Willow waited for him as he finished up the call and then a silence fell as he slid the phone into his pocket and turned, his midnight-blue eyes meeting hers.

She didn't look away. Couldn't, if truth was told. The sheer masculine beauty of him and his electrifying presence held her hypnotised. The air crackled between them, a shifting, twisting static charge, and her breath stopped in her throat. And for a second she thought he might stride straight across the space between them and take her in his arms. She wouldn't be sorry if he did, not at all.

But, of course, he didn't.

Instead he moved over to the great black slab of a desk that stood near the windows and leaned back against it, folding his arms, studying her.

'You really are quite the virgin sacrifice, aren't you?' he murmured.

For a second, Willow had no idea what he was talking about. Then she realised. 'Oh, you mean the white dress?' She kept her voice as cool as his. 'It was the first thing that came to hand.'

'I see.' His long, beautiful mouth curved. 'It's very appropriate.'

'I didn't wear it because it was appropriate. I wore it because it was too hot for jeans.'

He tilted his head, watching her. 'Is that a fact? Nothing at all to do with me, then?'

'Why would it have anything to do with you?'

'It's a lovely dress.' His smile took on a wicked edge. 'I can see right through it.'

Oh, dear. She hadn't thought of that, because it wasn't something she'd ever thought to check. She wore black trousers and a black T-shirt to work in the cafe, and she made sure they were clean when she dressed, but she'd never thought about whether her dresses were see-through or not.

Her cheeks heated, the spark of her temper igniting, and her instinct was to quell it and force it down. But, since she'd decided to give him a taste of the passion he said he wanted, for the first time in a long time Willow let it burn.

She met his gaze, held it, let him see her annoyance. 'Then perhaps you shouldn't be looking.'

The smile on his face slowly changed, losing its practised wickedness, and then he gave a genuine-sounding laugh. 'You're quite a contrary beast, aren't you, Diana?'

Contrary. Yes, she'd been told that many times, but usually in far more unflattering terms, such as oppositional and demanding, and difficult. And most often accompanied by a cold stare that made her feel small and stupid, as if there was something wrong with her.

But the Duke wasn't looking at her as if there was something wrong with her. He was looking at her as if he found her being contrary utterly delightful. And that didn't make her feel either small or stupid. It made her feel good.

It was an unfamiliar feeling and she didn't quite know how to deal with it, so she only shrugged. 'I'm not a beast and you can stop calling me Diana. My name is Willow.'

'Willow,' he echoed, as if tasting the sound of it and finding it delicious. 'It's a beautiful name, though you're not at all willow-like if I may say.' His gaze dropped slowly down the line of her figure, taking in every inch of her, a trail of sparks scorching her right through. 'You're far too fiery and strong for that.'

There was no doubt that he thought those were good things and that he liked them very much. It was clear in the heat in his eyes as they met hers.

That unfamiliar feeling in her chest, a kind of warmth, spread outwards, but she still didn't know how to deal with it, so she tried hard to ignore it. 'I'm nothing of the kind,' she said coolly. 'You wanted to discuss the wedding?'

'Straight to the point, aren't we?'

'I have some things I need to get back to.' Which was a lie. She had nothing at all to get back to.

He gave her a very direct look, which she met head-on, challenging him to call her out on it. And for a second she thought he might, but he only gestured to the long, low, black leather couch that stood near the desk. 'Please, take a seat.'

Willow moved over to the couch and sat, smoothing her dress over her knees.

'Would you care for coffee or tea?' he asked, all politeness. 'Or maybe even something a little more exciting? Champagne perhaps to toast our engagement?'

She blinked in surprise. 'Engagement?'

'Well, I can hardly marry you without an engagement,' he said as if it were self-evident. 'That wouldn't be proper at all.'

'I didn't think you cared about propriety.'

'Perhaps I've changed my mind.' He gave her a look from beneath his thick black lashes. 'Perhaps I do care about it after all, especially now I've decided to settle down.'

Willow found the conversation oddly discomforting, though she didn't know why. 'But you're not really settling down, are you?' she pointed out. 'You're paying me to be a wife and to have your child.'

His mouth curved in one of those sensual smiles that she was starting to see were quite practised. 'Yes, when you put it like that, it is rather cold and clinical. Perhaps that's why I'd like an engagement and a proper wedding. In a church. Perhaps I'd like people to think that it's real.'

She stared at him, trying to read the expression on his beautiful face. Trying to understand why he wanted all these things. Because they hadn't been in the contract she'd signed.

Why do you even care? What does it matter to you?

That was a good point. She didn't care if he wanted an engagement, or if he wanted a wedding in a church. Those things had no particular meaning for her. She was never going to have them anyway, since a real family and marriage wasn't on the cards.

So why the thought of them made something inside her ache a little she had no idea.

'Fine,' she said levelly, trying to sound disinterested. 'It doesn't matter to me.'

He frowned. 'You're very biddable all of a sudden, Diana. Why is that?'

A little shock went through her that he'd noticed. Then again, those eyes of his seemed to miss nothing.

She smoothed her dress again, not wanting to admit that the thought of an engagement and wedding made her uneasy, because she couldn't explain it even to herself, let alone him. 'Because you're clearly going to do whatever you want to do. Me arguing with you isn't going to change your mind.'

He lifted a brow. 'Do you want an engagement and wedding?'

'Surely it doesn't matter what I want?'

'Why would it not?'

She glared at him. 'Stop answering questions with questions.'

That much warmer, more genuine smile flickered around his mouth again. 'You're not at all afraid of me, are you?'

'Why would I be afraid of you?'

'Now who's answering questions with questions?'

She felt breathless all of a sudden, that smile touching something deep inside her. Something hot that she'd covered in a cold, hard shell.

'No,' she said. 'I'm not afraid of you.'

And his smile widened, as if that was something he liked, too. 'You should be, you know. I'm very rich and very powerful.' His voice deepened, taking on a sensual edge. 'And I'm also extremely notorious when it comes to women.'

Yes, he was. She'd read everything about him that she could lay her hands on. Research, of course. It wasn't at all because she found him unexpectedly fascinating.

'So I've heard.' She clasped her hands together to stop them from fidgeting. 'Again, nothing that would make me afraid of you. I do wonder, though, why you haven't answered my question. You're marrying because of a will, so why do you need a wedding when a quick ceremony in a register office would do the trick?'

'An interesting question.' He was very still, his lean, powerful body perfectly at rest, which somehow relaxed her, easing her urge to fidget. 'The fact is, I'm a very busy man. I work hard and then I play hard, and in the past that hasn't left a lot of time for other things. I hadn't thought a family would be important to me, but I admit that after my father died, that changed. I am the only Templeton left, and so I want a son to carry on after me.' Something she didn't understand shifted in his eyes. 'Would you really blame me if I wanted wedding pictures of his parents to show him when he got older?'

It certainly sounded good. Almost as if he believed every word he'd said. And yet she couldn't quite shake the feeling that he was spinning her a story. Not lying, she didn't think. More as if he wasn't giving her the whole truth.

'Wedding pictures?' She didn't bother to hide her disbelief. 'This is really all about wedding pictures?'

His expression was guileless. 'Oh, don't get me wrong. I wouldn't mind announcing to the world that I'm getting married also. It's not real if it isn't talked about on the internet somewhere, after all.'

Now, *that* he meant, she could tell.

'But it's not real,' she felt compelled to point out. 'I'm not marrying you because I'm in love with you.'

'Why should love make a difference?' There was an odd note in his voice that she couldn't quite interpret. 'But that doesn't matter anyway. In the eyes of the law our marriage will be as real as it gets, and the wedding is just the icing on the cake.' He gave her a sidelong look. 'Don't you want to wear a pretty dress?'

She ignored the question, studying the perfect lines of his face, trying to read the undercurrents in his voice and interpret the shadows shifting in his blue eyes. She wasn't sure why she found his motivations so interesting. Perhaps it was because they weren't obvious. Certainly he was turning out to be more complicated than she had thought, and she wasn't sure if that was a good thing or not. Probably not.

She didn't want to find him complicated. She didn't want him to be interesting.

She didn't want to be drawn to the still way he stood or feel warmth when he smiled at her.

Physical attraction she could deal with. Anything else, no.

'Keep staring at me, Diana,' he said softly, eyes gleaming. 'I like it very much.'

Her breath caught, yet another blush rising in her cheeks. She hadn't meant to be quite so obvious with her study, but then again, he was far too observant.

He gave another soft laugh, and before she could say anything he pushed himself abruptly away from his desk. 'Let me find Jane and we'll get some champagne in here. I want to do this properly.'

Willow wanted to tell him that there was no need, but he'd already pulled open the door and given some instructions to his PA. And then five minutes later, Jane bustled in with a bottle of what was clearly outrageously priced champagne and a couple of glasses on a silver tray. She deposited them on the table in front of Willow then bustled out again.

The Duke went around the side of the desk, pulled open a drawer, retrieved something from it then came over to where Willow sat.

The look in his eyes was hot, a blue flame that made it impossible for her to think.

Then, much to her shock, he dropped down onto one knee in a sudden, graceful movement. 'Don't look so surprised.' His smile was wicked and slightly mischievous, wholly seductive. 'I told you I wanted to do this properly.' He held out his hand, opening his fingers to reveal a small box of deep blue velvet. 'Willow Hall,' he said formally, 'will you do me the honour of becoming my wife?'

Willow stared at him uncertainly and a bit of him was pleased at how he'd managed to surprise her, disturb that cool, sharp front that was so at odds with the fire he could sense burning inside her.

And it was still there, that fire. He hadn't imagined it. Hadn't built it up over the space of the time since he'd seen her face-to-face into something it wasn't.

A contrary beast, he'd called her, and she was. Even now, sitting there on the couch in the most delicious white dress, she looked cool and collected, and totally self-contained.

Yet that dress was floaty and sheer, had a few little buttons at the front that were undone, revealing her light gold skin, and he could see the faint shadows of her knickers and bra beneath the fabric. And there was a certain energy to her, something kinetic, as if she could hardly keep from pushing herself off the couch and start pacing around.

He found the contrasts in her unexpectedly fascinating. How cool and still on the surface she was and yet how fiery and restless she was underneath.

He'd been a quiet, studious child himself, back before he'd realised how little that had mattered to his father, and some lost part of him was inexplicably drawn to her restlessness. It was bright as a star, flickering like a firefly, and he wanted to put out his hand to try and catch it.

In fact, Miss Willow Hall herself was proving to be a whole lot more intriguing and desirable to him than he'd first thought, which was not a bad thing.

The moment she'd walked into his office, oblivious to how lovely she was, her beautiful golden hair still in that wild ponytail that fell down her back, all he could think about was what she'd promised him—a wedding night. And as her gaze had met his, he'd known that she was thinking the same thing.

He'd been very tempted to throw caution to the wind and seduce her right here, right now. But he'd decided even before she'd arrived that he wasn't going to touch her again before their marriage. He was going to do everything in the proper order. Not quite what he was used to, yet anticipation wouldn't hurt and would make the night they eventually shared even more spectacular.

She stared at him and then at the little box in his hand, then reached out for it.

But he pulled it away before she could take it. 'Uh-huh. You have to give me your answer first.' He was teasing, of course, yet only for the pleasure of seeing the heat of her temper flare.

Obligingly it did, those golden sparks flickering in her eyes, which he found deeply satisfying. 'Of course I'm going to marry you. I've already told you I will. I even signed that wretched contract.'

'No, "I even signed that wretched contract" is not the right answer. Say "Yes, I'd love to be your wife, Temple".'

Her straight golden brows drew down. 'Why "Temple"? Is it just easier?'

It was not the question he'd expected to be asked, not at this important moment.

'No,' he said, a little irritation creeping into his tone, before trotting out his standard reply. 'Achilles has a weakness. I do not.'

'I see.' Her gaze was very sharp all of a sudden,

making him feel as if she'd somehow managed to prise off a piece of his armour to reveal the skin beneath it.

It was not a comfortable feeling and he wasn't sure how she'd managed it. He was usually the one who discomfited people, not the other way around.

'Well?' he demanded when she didn't say anything more. 'I can wait here all day if I have to.'

He didn't actually want to remain on one knee in front of her all day, and the fact that he'd even done it at all was something he didn't want to think about. But he wasn't a man who backed down, and she needed to understand that.

For a long moment they simply stared at each other and he thought that perhaps he *would* have to be stuck here all day, when she suddenly said, 'In that case I'd love to be your wife… Achilles.'

He didn't miss the deliberate use of his name. Just as he didn't miss the jolt of electricity that arrowed down his spine as she said it. The name he hated, because, as his mother had often told him, it was Ulysses' second name and so they'd given it to him, another burden he had to carry.

But it didn't sound like a burden when Willow said it. Instead it sounded sensual and sexy, and it made him hard.

You're letting her get to you.

No, he wasn't. So he liked her saying his name? It didn't mean anything. And if it made him hard, then again, what of it? It was only going to make their wedding night even better.

He inclined his head in acknowledgement of his

name, but gave her no other sign of how it affected him, because that was another bit of power he didn't want to give her.

Instead he allowed her to take the box out of his hand, waiting as she lifted the lid.

A ring sat in the midnight-blue velvet. A beautiful, clear yellow diamond in a heavy white gold band set with tiny smaller white diamonds.

He watched her face as she stared at the ring, conscious of how the satisfaction inside him became heavier, settling down to lie deep in his bones, becoming a certainty.

The diamond was the exact shade of her eyes, just as he knew it would be.

The ring destined for his brother's bride.

'This is…beautiful,' she said huskily. 'I can't—'

'You can.' Because he would have this. 'It was my mother's engagement ring, and my grandmother's before her. All Audley brides wear it.'

'I…'

He took the box from her, discarding it on the floor as he extracted the ring. Then he reached for her hand and gently slid it onto her finger.

It fitted perfectly.

Her skin was warm on his and when she looked at him he felt another electric shock of desire go through him, along with an intense feeling of possession. As if he'd known all along, even from the moment he'd seen her by the lake, that this woman was destined to be his.

Perhaps it should have disturbed him, because he'd

never once felt the slightest twinge of possessiveness over a woman before. He simply hadn't cared enough.

But he wasn't disturbed. It felt right. It felt as if it was meant to be.

Colour rose in her cheeks, a deep and pretty pink, as if she knew exactly what he was thinking. And he thought that might make her jerk her hand from his and walk straight out of his office.

But she didn't. Instead her gaze dropped to his mouth, and suddenly everything slowed down, time becoming thick and syrupy as honey.

Her gaze flicked up to hold his, golden as the diamond on her finger and just as full of glitter and sparks. Then she leaned forward and lightly, so lightly, as if testing, brushed her mouth over his.

He didn't move, didn't breathe. Her kiss went through him like light, like the dawn breaking over frozen-solid ground. A warm ray of sun, heating him up, melting him. And he almost moved. Almost reached for her and pulled her to the floor of his office, almost gave in to his own hunger, the depth of which he hadn't guessed at till now.

Almost.

But there was still a part of him that wouldn't countenance such a loss of control and so he remained on one knee, frozen where he was on the floor, his hands curled into fists as her lips brushed over his and then away.

Her gaze was molten, smoky with heat, and he thought that perhaps the kiss had pushed her to the edge, just as it had pushed him. And that maybe she wanted him to keep on pushing, because there was a distinct challenge in her eyes.

But no, he wasn't going to let her goad him into it. A wedding night he'd demanded and a wedding night he'd have. And that would happen when *he* wanted it to happen, not her.

So Achilles smiled at her, letting her know that he could see what she was trying to do, and that it wouldn't work. Then he rose to his feet and moved unhurriedly over to the coffee table where the champagne and glasses were.

She didn't say anything. Yet he could feel the pressure of her gaze on his back.

Had he made her hungrier? Made her mad? He hoped so. That fire in her burned so bright and he wanted it so very badly.

He grabbed the champagne bottle and popped the cork, forcing aside the desire that gripped him, concentrating instead on the feeling of satisfaction. Everything was going exactly according to his plan and that gave him an inordinate amount of pleasure.

Pouring out a couple of glasses, he then carried them over to where Willow sat and handed her one. She gave it a faintly suspicious glance, then took it.

He raised his own glass and tapped it against hers. 'Here's to our marriage.'

She gave a little nod then took a sip of the fizzing liquid. 'So, you wanted to discuss the wedding?'

'Indeed I did. I see no point in waiting, so the ceremony will take place next week at the church in Thornhaven village. Then we will honeymoon in Greece, at my villa on Heiros.'

She blinked. 'Next week?'

'You have a better time?'

'Oh, no, I just didn't expect it to be so soon.' She frowned. 'But…a honeymoon?'

Ah, he might have known he wouldn't be able to slip that one by her. She was too sharp for that.

He shoved one hand in his pocket and sipped at his champagne. 'Of course a honeymoon,' he said casually.

'Why would we need a honeymoon?'

'Don't you want to go to Greece?'

'Stop distracting me. That's not what I asked.'

He didn't particularly want to confess this part of his plan to her, but she would find out soon enough. Because yes, she was far too sharp not to guess his intentions. And it had been something that he'd been considering for the past couple of days as he'd taken charge of the wedding preparations.

'Very well.' He met her gaze head-on. 'I decided on a honeymoon because I fully intend to seduce you into extending our wedding night to at least a week.'

Her eyes widened, and her mouth opened, then shut.

So he went on, 'You want to conceive our child via medical assistance, but if we're going to have one night anyway, then we might as well use that to try for a baby. And if we're going to do that, then why not extend that to a week while we're away?' He smiled. 'It makes perfect logical sense, don't you see?'

At least, it had made perfect logical sense to him. One night wasn't going to be enough, not with the kind of heat they generated between them, and, since they had a child to conceive, they may as well make use of that heat to its fullest extent.

'Yes,' she said at last, her voice more than a touch hoarse. 'I do see.'

It was clear she was shocked and more than a little uneasy, and it made something tighten uncomfortably in his chest. What was it about sex that disturbed her so much? The kisses they'd shared earlier she'd enjoyed, she'd told him as much. And even just now, she'd kissed him and there had been clear desire in her eyes. So it wasn't him.

Had she had a bad experience with someone else, though? Was that why she'd remained a virgin?

Why are you so interested? What does it matter?

Perhaps it didn't matter. After all, they weren't going to stay married long. Yet the tightness in his chest intensified, a surge of something that felt like anger going through him. Whether it mattered or not, he didn't like the thought of her being hurt. He didn't like it at all.

'I won't force you,' he said with quiet emphasis. 'Understand that right now. I would never do that to you or to any woman. If you don't want me, you only need to say.'

More surprise flickered over her face and she looked away, clearly flustered. 'I'm…that's not what…' She trailed off and was silent a moment. Then she said, 'I said I would give you a wedding night and I meant it.'

'But you're reluctant.'

She said nothing, taking another sip of her drink.

'Why?' His own drink was forgotten as interest

grabbed onto him. 'Did someone hurt you? Did someone—?'

'No.' The word was sharp. 'No, nothing like that. I just…' She stopped again. 'I haven't felt this way before. About anyone.'

The admission was hesitant and for a second he didn't understand it. 'You mean…desire?'

Slowly, she nodded. 'I haven't met anyone I wanted before. Not like this.' There was a brilliant flash of gold as she glanced at him. 'Not like…you.'

He didn't know why that hit him the way it did, like a short, sharp punch to the chest. Maybe it was because no one had ever said that to him before. Oh, women wanted him. Women went out of their way to make that very clear. But none of them had ever told him they'd never wanted anyone else but him.

It was only physical desire, he knew that. It didn't mean anything. And yet he felt as if it did all the same. Because for the first time in his entire life, someone wanted *him*. Not his money, not his power, not his reputation. Not even his skill in bed.

She hadn't known about any of those things when she'd seen him by the lake, and yet she'd wanted him.

You. Not Ulysses.

It shouldn't matter. It shouldn't have anything to do with Ulysses.

But it did matter. It mattered a lot.

'That frightens you?' he asked, watching her.

'No. It…it means that…' Her fingers around her glass were clenched, her other hand gripping the material of her dress. The restless energy to her seemed to increase, and he'd crossed the space between them before he could think better of it, taking the glass from her suddenly shaking hand and putting it down, then holding both her hands in his and instinctively squeezing gently to calm her.

Her gaze dropped, but she didn't pull away or stiffen up. She just looked at her hands in his and slowly her agitation began to ebb away.

'I'm difficult, Achilles,' she said in a low voice at last, her gaze still on their linked hands. 'I have a very bad temper as you probably saw last week, and I don't lose it very often, but when I do I can…hurt people.' The flush to her cheeks had become more intense, but this time he knew it wasn't hunger. It was shame. 'When I'm pushed or challenged, it gets worse, and it seems you have that unfortunate effect on me.' She looked up at him suddenly, a raw honesty in her eyes. 'I'll certainly try not to be difficult after we're married, but when I'm around you…well, I can't guarantee anything.'

He had not expected such candour. Hadn't expected his own reaction to it either, and it was clear from the look on her face that it had cost her.

But he couldn't imagine her hurting anyone. Yes, she was fiery and yes, she'd lifted a hand to him, but he had provoked her. And the electricity between them surely hadn't helped. She didn't seem a woman liable to flying off the handle, though, not when she'd seemed very cool around him—when he wasn't provoking her, of course.

What had happened to make her think it was an

issue? And why did she call herself difficult? She hadn't seemed difficult to him. A woman of deep passions, perhaps, but not difficult.

He wanted to ask her questions, find out why she thought these things about herself, but he didn't want to make her distressed or agitated more than she already was. Perhaps there would be some time later, when they were on honeymoon.

You don't need to know. Why would you want to?

Achilles shoved that thought away. 'Diana, I handle extremely difficult people every day. One fiery, passionate goddess is nothing.'

She frowned, even as the remaining tension in her seemed to die away. 'I'm not a goddess.'

'Let me be the judge of that.' He gave her fingers another squeeze then let them go. 'Now, let's discuss something less problematic for a change. What are your thoughts on wedding gowns?'

CHAPTER SIX

OVER THE COURSE of the next week, as arrangements for the wedding began in earnest, Willow wondered from time to time if her confession in Achilles' office had been a mistake. She'd never been so honest with another person before—she'd never had any kind of personal discussion with anyone before—and part of her had been very reluctant to confess to anything.

But she could tell that he wasn't going to let her reluctance go when it came to a physical relationship. He was too observant to lie to and too experienced for made-up excuses. He knew she wanted him, she'd as good as told him, and so of course her clear agitation about the thought of sex was going to make him curious.

She couldn't bear for him to assume things, either, or think that the issue was him when it wasn't. Or rather, it *was* him, but not for the reasons he thought.

So truth had seemed to be the best option.

She hadn't known what to expect when she'd told him about her terrible temper—some offhanded, casual comment perhaps. A shrug. Or maybe even distaste, because he didn't seem a man given to overly emotional displays himself.

What she hadn't expected at all was for him to put his wine down and come over to her and take her suddenly shaking hands in his. And she hadn't realised how agitated she'd been until that moment.

His hold had been warm and firm, feeling strangely like an anchor keeping her in place, and his attention had been wholly on her as she'd told him, his gaze direct yet without judgement. And it hadn't felt as hard to confess such a terrible weakness as she'd first thought.

She'd thought he might ask her whom she'd hurt in the past with her anger, and she hadn't wanted to tell him about her father, about the last precious photo of her mother that she'd torn up because she'd been so furious. Or about how her normally shut-down father had looked at her as if she'd stabbed him, and then clutched at his head and collapsed in front of her.

He'd nearly died that night. The doctors had told her that his stroke could have happened at any time, but she knew it was because of her. Because she'd ripped up the last photo he had of his beloved wife in a fury. Because she'd hurt him and had wanted to hurt him.

Luckily, though, Achilles hadn't asked her and so she at least hadn't had to confess that crime to him, and she'd been more than happy to move on to discussing gowns and other less fraught subjects.

He hadn't pursued the topic, clearly busy with wedding arrangements. He'd made various gracious invitations for her to join in with the decision-making process, which she just as graciously declined.

She didn't want to be involved in it. The whole thing was a pointless performance, though part of her was curious as to whom exactly he was performing for. She certainly didn't believe he'd suddenly decided on a formal engagement, complete with ring, plus a wedding and honeymoon, just for some photos.

No, it was about something more than that, but she tried to put it out of her mind. The very last thing she wanted was to become curious about her notorious playboy husband-to-be.

He did have her try on numerous wedding dresses before finally approving some white silk and tulle concoction, accented with gilt thread, that Willow told herself she didn't care about. Yet at the same time, as she looked at herself in the mirror, she was conscious of a strange ache somewhere deep inside her.

She'd never thought a husband and children would be for her, and yet here she was, about to commit herself to both. That it wasn't real, she knew. But that didn't change the small ache inside her, the tug of longing for something…more.

But that was dangerous, so she ignored it.

In between wedding-dress fittings and investigating degree programmes at various universities, she found herself casually looking up Achilles on the internet, despite telling herself that she really didn't need to know anything about him.

Apparently though, some part of her was desperate for information, hungrily combing through search results for anything interesting.

There were lots of news reports of how he'd left

home at sixteen with nothing and then made a lot of money in investment and venture capital. How he'd cut a swathe through the female population of Europe and then the States, apparently not caring one iota about his family or his reputation.

His father had publicly repudiated him from all accounts, not that it made any difference to Achilles; he was famously reported for saying, when asked about his father, 'Who?' That of course piqued Willow's curiosity. The two had not got on, it was clear, and naturally she wanted to know why.

So she'd focused her research deeper, on Andrew Templeton and his lovely Greek wife, Katerina. They'd apparently had a perfect marriage and been deeply in love, and not long after their wedding they'd had a son they named Ulysses. There were lots of pictures of the happy family, the lovely wife, the handsome Duke and their adorable little boy.

And then she came across a news item that made her gut lurch.

Ulysses had contracted meningitis when he was fifteen and had died very quickly. The Duke and his Duchess had been devastated. And then a year after their first son's death, they'd had another child. Achilles.

Willow found that puzzling for reasons she couldn't quite pinpoint, the first son's death and then Achilles' birth so soon afterwards. Almost as if the Duke and Duchess had tried to replace the son they'd lost. Clearly whatever healing they'd attempted hadn't worked, because five years after Achilles' birth, his mother had divorced the Duke and returned to Athens, leaving her son behind, and had died a few years later.

It was obvious that neither the Duke nor the Duchess had got over the death of their first son, and it made her wonder what kind of childhood Achilles had had with that kind of shadow hanging over his head.

And then she thought about the wedding he was planning, the engagement with the family heirloom on her finger, the honeymoon in his mother's country…

It's definitely not for you.

The ache inside her, the one she told herself she didn't feel, deepened, though it shouldn't. Because she knew he wasn't marrying her for her. That it was all for whatever point he was trying to prove—and he was trying to prove a point, that was obvious. Though to whom, she didn't know.

Whatever, she needed not to feel the ache. Becoming emotionally invested was dangerous for her, and if she'd learned anything by now it was that.

She had to keep her distance. Shut herself off. Lock herself down.

And your wedding night? The honeymoon he wants from you?

She remembered back in his office how his presence had made her feel restless and wound up, and then not long after that how his touch had calmed her. There had been something still in him that had then stilled her, and she'd found it…restful.

It was strange that he could be both calming and arousing, but maybe that would help come their wedding night. Because the more she thought about it, the

YOU pick your books –
WE pay for everything.
You get up to FOUR New Books and
TWO Mystery Gifts...absolutely FREE

Dear Reader,

I am writing to announce the launch of a huge **FREE BOOKS GIVEAWAY**... and to let you know that YOU are entitled to choose up to FOUR fantastic books that WE pay for.

Try **Harlequin® Desire** books featuring the worlds of the American elite with juicy plot twists, delicious sensuality and intriguing scandal.

Try **Harlequin Presents® Larger-Print** books featuring the glamourous lives of royals and billionaires in a world of exotic locations, where passion knows no bounds.

Or TRY BOTH!

In return, we ask just one favor: Would you please participate in our brief Reader Survey? We'd love to hear from you.

This FREE BOOKS GIVEAWAY means that we pay for *everything!* We'll even cover the shipping, and no purchase is necessary, now or later. So please return your survey today. You'll get **Two Free Books** and **Two Mystery Gifts** from each series to try, altogether worth over **$20!**

Sincerely

Pam Powers

Pam Powers
For Harlequin Reader Service

Complete the survey below and return it today to receive up to 4 FREE BOOKS and FREE GIFTS guaranteed!

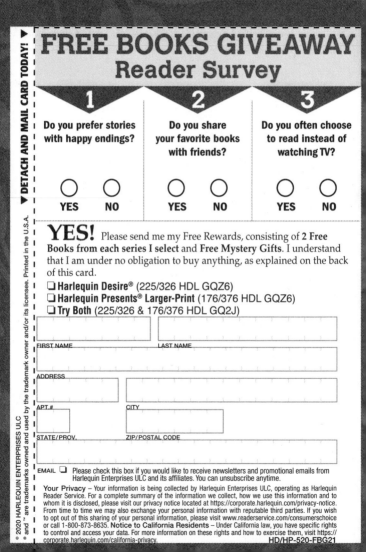

▼ DETACH AND MAIL CARD TODAY! ▼

FREE BOOKS GIVEAWAY
Reader Survey

1

Do you prefer stories with happy endings?

○ YES ○ NO

2

Do you share your favorite books with friends?

○ YES ○ NO

3

Do you often choose to read instead of watching TV?

○ YES ○ NO

YES! Please send me my Free Rewards, consisting of **2 Free Books from each series I select** and **Free Mystery Gifts**. I understand that I am under no obligation to buy anything, as explained on the back of this card.

❑ Harlequin Desire® (225/326 HDL GQZ6)
❑ Harlequin Presents® Larger-Print (176/376 HDL GQZ6)
❑ Try Both (225/326 & 176/376 HDL GQ2J)

FIRST NAME

LAST NAME

ADDRESS

APT.#

CITY

STATE/PROV.

ZIP/POSTAL CODE

EMAIL ❑ Please check this box if you would like to receive newsletters and promotional emails from Harlequin Enterprises ULC and its affiliates. You can unsubscribe anytime.

HD/HP-520-FBG21

HARLEQUIN® Reader Service — **Here's how it works:**

BUSINESS REPLY MAIL
FIRST-CLASS MAIL   PERMIT NO. 717   BUFFALO, NY

POSTAGE WILL BE PAID BY ADDRESSEE

HARLEQUIN READER SERVICE
PO BOX 1341
BUFFALO NY 14240-8571

NO POSTAGE
NECESSARY
IF MAILED
IN THE
UNITED STATES

more she wanted it. Perhaps it would even help. It could be like a safety valve, helping her let off steam in the same way being in the woods had helped her let off steam as a child.

The day of the wedding arrived all too soon.

Willow found her little bedroom in the cottage full of make-up artists and stylists, people poking and prodding her until she finally emerged in the beautiful tulle and silk wedding gown, her face immaculate, her hair braided in a crown around her head and threaded through with flowers, a shimmering veil in gilt lace thrown over the top.

She barely had a moment to look at the stranger in the mirror before she was whisked downstairs and into the black limo that would take her from the cottage to the little church in Thornhaven village.

The church was historic, Norman age, and packed with people. The press waited outside, cameras at the ready as Willow got out of the limo. They called her name as she went up the old church's steps, shouting questions at her as she went, but by that stage Achilles' PA, Jane, was there, helping her with her gown and flowers, whispering in her ear to just ignore them.

She tried, but it was all very strange. The whole situation was strange. Dressed in white and ready to marry a man she didn't love in front of a big crowd of people she didn't know, and all because she needed the money and her father taken care of.

A business arrangement, Achilles had assured her. Yet it didn't feel like a business arrangement any more.

Not when there was a gown and an engagement ring, and a church. Not when there was a honeymoon.

All the trappings of love without the emotion.

A bit like your life, isn't it?

Willow clutched her bouquet, waiting for the music to start for her walk down the aisle. Conscious that the place at her side was empty. Because the place at her side, where her father should have been, was always empty.

He hadn't wanted to walk down the aisle with her because he wasn't physically steady enough, and he'd said it wasn't real anyway so it didn't matter that he wasn't there. He'd gone to Europe, to get the treatment paid for by the Duke.

He's never been a real father to you anyway. All the trappings without the emotion.

A lump rose in her throat. She'd loved her father, but he hadn't loved her. He'd never said it to her, hadn't ever demonstrated it to her. She'd been the baby he hadn't wanted, the child that had ruined his career. A lasting reminder of what his beloved wife had wanted and didn't survive long enough to have.

He'd done his duty by her, given her a roof over her head and food on the table, ensured she had a decent education, and as soon as the Duke's money had arrived he'd left.

Perhaps he was right, though. Perhaps it didn't matter. Perhaps it was fine that this was all for show and that none of it was for her.

Nothing ever had been, after all.

Well, not quite nothing.

There was *one* thing that was for her and he waited for her by the altar, exquisitely dressed in a morning suit of dove grey. The man who might not love her, but did want her, and certainly enough to demand a wedding night from her.

That gave her some courage as she walked towards him, as did the look in his midnight eyes, full of a strangely intense satisfaction and fierce possessiveness that she didn't quite understand.

It might have been the look of a man desperately in love who was finally marrying the woman of his dreams. Except she knew that wasn't true, that he didn't dream about her. That all of this was simply a show that he was putting on, and she was merely part of it.

But then there was no time to think too deeply as the ceremony began, so she pushed it aside, concentrating instead on remembering the lines she had to say. And then before she knew it, Achilles' ring was on her finger and her veil was being pushed aside as he bent slightly to kiss her.

People were smiling and clapping as she walked out of the church on her new husband's arm, photographers clamouring, confetti in the air. She smiled reflexively at no one in particular as Achilles walked with her down the church steps to the long black limo that waited for them at the side of the road.

And then she was in the car, the door slamming shut behind them like the vault of a crypt, and she was finally alone with Achilles.

She turned to look at him, but the moment he'd got

in the car he'd pulled out his phone and was now talking to someone in liquid Greek.

Her husband.

She looked down at her hands clasped on the white silk of her gown, the yellow diamond sparkling, the heavy gold band of her wedding ring a perfect complement.

You're married.

Yes, she was. But it didn't mean anything. All that it meant was that now…

You get your wedding night.

Her breath caught, everything tightening inside her. She could still feel the warmth of his mouth as she'd leaned in to kiss him that day of their engagement, that ring heavy on her finger. Unable to stop herself. Drawn inexorably to him by the heat in his eyes and the hunger that she couldn't escape.

He'd been so still as her mouth had brushed over his and she'd wanted very much to make him move, to get him to reach for her, perhaps pull her down onto the carpet of his office and show her everything a man could do to a woman to give her pleasure.

But he hadn't.

As soon as she'd lifted her mouth from his, he'd risen to his feet and moved away as if nothing had happened. As if she hadn't shaken him as completely as he'd shaken her.

Perhaps tonight she'd rectify that.

Are you sure that's wise?

Well, maybe not. But then, she'd told him that she was difficult. He'd been warned. And he hadn't looked all that perturbed about it, either, telling her he dealt with difficult people every day, which was probably true, given his business dealings.

But were they more difficult than her? Had any of them nearly killed their father?

Achilles abruptly disconnected the call and pocketed his phone, turning his head and meeting her stare. And a familiar heat washed through her at the intense look in his blue gaze.

Yes, this was for her. *He* was for her.

The thought made a cold, hard knot in the centre of her chest loosen slightly.

'Don't worry, Diana.' His tone was lazy, at odds with the look in his eyes, and he reached for her hand, bringing it to his lips and brushing a kiss over the back of it. 'I'm not going to ravage you now, though believe me, I'm very tempted. I have other plans.'

She shivered at the light touch and at the heat curling through her. 'I assume a reception?'

'Oh, there's a reception, certainly. Except we will not be attending. We will be elsewhere.'

'I see. And where will we be?'

Achilles leaned back in his seat and smiled. 'We will be on our way to Greece.'

She lifted a brow. 'Honeymoon already?'

'Of course. I didn't want to wait. We're headed to the airport now and the jet will take us to Athens and then on to Heiros, a little island not too far from Santorini.' His eyes gleamed. 'I thought you might appreciate some sun.'

It struck her then, almost forcibly, that, while everything else might have been for show, the honeymoon wasn't. He didn't need it to fulfil the terms of the will. All he'd needed was her name on the marriage licence and eventually a child.

The honeymoon had been because he wanted her.

Not just anyone. *Her.*

There were so many reasons why she shouldn't let that matter to her, so many reasons why it shouldn't be important, but right now, with a ring that didn't mean anything on her finger and wearing a wedding gown that was just for show, it did feel important.

The hard, cold knot in her chest unravelled completely.

'Yes.' She smiled, something she hadn't done in far too long. 'I think I would appreciate that very much.'

They took a helicopter to London and, from there, Achilles' private jet to Athens. Somehow a passport had been got for her, as had several suitcases that apparently contained all she would need for a honeymoon in Greece.

No one batted an eyelid at her wedding gown as she boarded the jet, but by then she'd long got over any self-consciousness. There were too many other things to look at. The novelty of being on a plane, for example, and the excitement of take-off and landing. The view through the windows of the world beneath them and the glimmer and glint of cities as they soared over the continent.

Willow forgot about trying to be distant and cool, too busy alternately staring out of the window and leafing through a magazine about the Greek Islands, all the while firing questions at Achilles lounging opposite her. He looked ostensibly as lazy as a sleepy panther, but every so often, when he looked at her, she could see the glow of blue deep in his gaze. A hungry glow.

It was exciting. It made her want to get up and go to him herself, see what he'd do if she kissed him, if she laid her hands on him. But despite everything, she still felt a little shy, so she didn't.

A few hours later they landed in Athens, only to be taken to a helicopter that flew them straight out across the Aegean and to Heiros, Achilles' private island.

The villa was the most perfect house Willow had ever seen. It was built of white stone and perched high on a clifftop overlooking the sea, and walking into it felt like walking into the interior of a cloud. The inside was white, white walls and a white stone floor, nothing to compete with the views of the intense blue sea outside, the rocky cliffs and the deep green trees clinging to those cliffs. The couches and chairs were all deep and cushioned, covered with white linen, and colourful cushions were scattered here and there.

The outside of the villa was wrapped in ivy and there was a stone terrace that led straight out from the front living area, shaded by an ivy-covered pergola.

Willow, drawn by the view, stepped straight onto the terrace, looking down to see a path cut into the rocky cliffside that led to a pool that had also been cut into the cliffside. The water was as blue as the sea below it and incredibly inviting...

It was so different to Yorkshire, the house she'd grown up in and the forests around Thornhaven. This was all blue sea and rocky cliffs and heat, while York-shire was green and cold and rainy.

It was so beautiful. She wanted to stay here for ever.

In the villa behind her, she heard Achilles speaking to his staff as they carried in the last of the bags, and then the door closing behind them as they left.

There was no one else here, just her and Achilles.

Her mouth dried, her heartbeat suddenly picking up. The air around her was warm, smelling of salt from the sea, and she could hear the cry of the gulls in the air.

And then she felt his hands settle lightly on her hips, the heat of his body right behind her. 'And now, Diana,' Achilles murmured in her ear, 'I believe I owe you a wedding night.'

He'd been good the whole day. Right from the moment she'd stepped into the church and he'd watched her walk up the aisle to him, a vision in white and silver gilt.

The gown had been perfect, her hair a braided golden crown on her head, threaded through with flowers and covered by a silvery veil. His tall goddess now a fairy queen.

The cream of society had watched her marry him. In the church where his own parents had been married and where Ulysses had been christened. He'd been christened there too, but that had been before his parents had realised that he would never replace the boy they'd lost. That he didn't measure up. That he was faulty.

His father had told him the night of his sixteenth birthday, after Achilles had handed him the scholar's prize he'd won for his year, hoping to impress him, that it didn't matter what marks he got. It didn't matter how good at school he was, or how impressed his teachers were with him. None of that mattered. The only thing that did was that he was supposed to be Ulysses. Ulysses, who had been good at rugby and who'd loved going fishing with his father in the lake. Who had wanted to go hunting and who had already been learning how to use a rifle and was a crack shot.

Ulysses, who'd been good at everything that Achilles wasn't.

That was the night that his father had also mentioned that the only reason Achilles had been born was to replace the son they'd lost. Ulysses was the heir, Achilles the spare. And the spare was all he'd ever be, because the heir had gone and nothing could replace him.

And that was also the night that Achilles had left Thornhaven with nothing but the clothes on his back and his passport. He'd gone to Greece, but not to find his mother—she'd died years earlier, and besides, it had been obvious what her choice had been the day she'd divorced his father and left without looking back. He'd wanted to get away from England, get away from his father and the constant hope that refused to die that one day his father would let Ulysses go. That Andrew Templeton would move on from his grief and love the son he had just as much as he loved the one who'd died.

But it was a hope that had never materialised and so he'd killed that hope stone dead.

He wanted to build his own life on his own terms,

to not feel like a ghost haunting the rooms of his own house, pouring himself into filling a dead boy's shoes.

But things had changed now. His father's will had changed it, and now the woman meant for Ulysses was his, and he was going to make that true in every possible way there was.

He couldn't wait. He'd been dreaming of this the whole week, of having her to himself. Of taking her here to his island and unleashing her fire. He wanted to know what it would look like and how it would feel. Whether she'd be as difficult as she'd said she was, and oh, he hoped so. He was desperate to match himself against her, watch her ignite, watch her blaze. And for him. Just for him.

Gently he tugged her back against him, so that she was pressed against the length of his body. She was soft, the sweet scent of her winding around him. He had been fantasising about peeling that dress from her, then unbraiding the crown of golden hair on her head, the flowers woven into it scattering everywhere.

Greece was the territory he'd claimed for himself rather than the estate where he'd always felt like an interloper, and so bringing her here appealed to his sense of possessiveness. A good decision, he thought as the breeze from the sea stirred her veil, bringing the scent of salt and sunshine. There were no ghosts in Greece. Of course, there was his mother, but she was long gone, and anyway, she'd lived in Athens.

He felt Willow tremble slightly and then she turned around, looking up at him.

There was something in her expression he couldn't

read. It reminded him of that day in his office, when she'd become so tense, and he'd taken hold of her hands, and she'd told him that he had to be careful of her.

'What is it?' he asked, cupping one cheek in his palm, her skin warm and silky to the touch. 'Are you afraid? I won't hurt you, Diana. I know what I'm doing when it comes to pleasure.'

She shook her head, yet he could feel the tension in her body. Could see it in her golden-brown eyes. She stared at him. 'This…this is for me, isn't it? The honeymoon. Because you wanted me.'

There was a raw edge to her voice, a glitter in those beautiful eyes. Wanting it to be true and yet…afraid that it wasn't.

He remembered that feeling. Every time he'd looked at his father, hoping that this would be the day that it wouldn't be Ulysses he saw when he looked at Achilles. That this would be the day he'd finally feel like his father's son and not the ghost he'd been made into.

But his father had never looked at him that way, and now he never would.

You'll always remain a ghost.

Achilles forced away the thought, stared down into the fear in Willow's eyes, and he knew that there was no part of him that could lie to her. Or to himself.

Of course this was for her. He could have bedded her in Thornhaven straight after the wedding if it had simply been about claiming her. If it had all been about taking his dead brother's promised wife.

But it wasn't just about that. It was about her. Willow. His golden goddess. About the chemistry that leapt between them. About the way she made him feel, as if there was fire inside of him too instead of only ashes and shadows.

And she was here because he wanted her to ignite him, just as he wanted to ignite her. It was about sex, yes. But he couldn't pretend it was only about that. If it had been, the master suite at Thornhaven would have sufficed. He wouldn't have brought her here, to the place where he felt the most alive, and for an entire week.

You cannot make this mean anything.

Achilles stroked his thumb over the satiny skin of her cheekbone. Oh, it wouldn't mean anything, no fear of that. Though it was perhaps a little deeper than purely physical, it wasn't much deeper.

His emotions, such as they were, were shallow things, and shallow was where they needed to stay.

'Yes,' he said, no seductiveness in his voice now. 'This is for you. Because I want you. But don't make it mean anything.' He stared down at her, watching the currents shift and turn in her eyes, knowing he had to say it. That he had to make it clear so there could be no misunderstandings. 'What is between us is physical only. Nothing more.'

Some fleeting emotion he couldn't read flickered through her gaze, then was gone. 'Yes.' Her voice sounded thick. 'I understand.'

'Good.' Achilles slid his thumb across her cheek again, brushing the corner of her lovely mouth. 'And

I want a week, wife of mine. Not just one night. Will you give me that?'

She looked at him for one long, uncounted second. And then she abruptly rose on her toes and pressed her mouth to his.

The smouldering fire inside him ignited.

The taste of blackberries and sunshine filled his head, a bright explosion of sweet and tart, and suddenly he couldn't think. It felt as if he'd been waiting half his life for this moment, for her mouth under his and the sweet taste of her on his tongue.

He wanted more. And he wanted it now.

Everything fell away. His father. His brother. His mother. All the pain in his heart that he told himself he didn't feel and all the anger underneath it. The creeping sense that he had sometimes that he was the one who had died, not Ulysses.

All of it was gone. There was only this. Only her. Her sweet mouth and the heat that leapt between them. And the hunger that followed hard on its heels.

He'd had plans for her. Plans to make this special, to go slow and take his time. Ease the trepidation he'd sensed in her the week before in his office. Gradually coax her flame high and hot, and only then would he take her.

But all those plans burned to ashes on the ground.

Fabric ripped as he clawed her gown from her, buttons scattering on the stone floor of the terrace. He wasn't seductive or sensual. He was a beast as he tore away the material and then pulled at the fragile lace of her underwear.

She didn't protest, her entire body shivering as he bared her, her mouth as hot and hungry as his, her arms tight around his neck as she pressed herself against him.

Yes, he'd had plans. A wide, soft bed upstairs strewn with rose petals, and champagne to toast their marriage.

Instead he barely had enough time to get her to the living room. He laid her down on the couch, her body long and lithe and a pale, creamy gold. Slender thighs and shapely hips. High, perfect breasts with the prettiest pink nipples. A soft nest of golden curls between her legs. Utterly and completely beautiful.

He didn't pause to look at her, to appreciate her the way he'd planned. He didn't stroke her to ease any nervousness she might have had. He didn't kiss his way down her body the way he should have, or murmur seductive praise as he did so.

Because she reached up to him and pulled him down, her mouth demanding on his, and then he was pushing her thighs apart while clawing at his zip. Getting his suit trousers undone and getting himself ready.

And then he positioned himself.

He should have waited then, should have tried to build even the smallest amount of anticipation.

But it was beyond him.

Then she wound her arms around his neck, arched her back, closed her legs around his waist and he was pushing inside her, and then there was nothing but fire.

She shuddered, gasping against his mouth, her hips lifting against his, trembling.

He kissed her harder, deeper, tasting her, exploring her. She felt so hot around him, so slick. Clasping him so tightly. Her body was a wonder, silky and smooth, and he felt his grip on reality loosen.

He began to move, an insistent, demanding rhythm, slipping a hand beneath the small of her back, guiding her to match him. And she did. Her kiss became feverish, her legs around his waist tightening.

He felt feverish himself, half-crazed. He moved harder, deeper, faster. Her scent was around him, sweet and musky, and somehow her hair had come down from its braided crown and was in his hands. There were flowers scattered all around them, crushed between them and scenting the air.

And, as he'd thought, she was fire in his hands and she was burning. And so was he. Fire and magic, and raw, intense pleasure. It was everything that had been missing from his life and he hadn't even known until this moment. Everything he had never thought he wanted.

Her passion made him real, somehow. Made him feel as if he existed, as if he was alive. Truly alive, not just going through the motions of it.

You want more than a week.

The thought was crystal in his brain, sharp edges and glittering planes.

And then she writhed beneath him, her teeth closing demandingly on his bottom lip, and the thought exploded into sparkling shards in his brain.

There was no thought any more, only the most primitive of physical responses and the pleasure that spun like molten mercury through every part of him, searing him straight through.

He moved inside her, driving them on, and there was no time to savour. No time for anticipation or for being lazy and easy. There was only the fire of her and her gasps of pleasure in his ear, the hoarse demands she made.

Her nails dug into him, and he had enough of himself left to ease a hand between them, down to where they were joined, giving her her pleasure first. And then as she cried his name, he took his own.

It came for him in a blaze of light, the bonfire of her rising up around him, consuming him. And he flung himself into the flames and burned himself to ash in her arms.

CHAPTER SEVEN

WILLOW LAY BENEATH ACHILLES, panting, feeling as if every part of her had shattered and then been put together in a strange and new and wonderful way.

Pleasure echoed through her like the tolling of some vast bell, a pulsing deep inside that made her shiver and shake. And for a second all she felt was wonder. His weight was heavy on her, but she didn't feel crushed. She could hear his breathing, as fast as hers, and she swore she could almost hear the thudding of his heart too.

She'd never been this close to anyone before, not physically, and the feeling of being surrounded and contained made her feel calm and safe, and relaxed for the first time in what felt like years.

So different to how she'd felt out on the terrace, where a sudden burst of fear had taken her. That somehow being here on this beautiful island was for show too, that she'd misunderstood, and that all of this wasn't for her after all. Even that he didn't want her as much as he'd implied.

She'd had to know. So she'd turned and looked up

into his dark blue eyes, and asked him straight out. But the truth had been there in his gaze and in the heat of his body, in the stroke of his thumb across her cheek. Desire burned there and she knew it was for her.

This was only physical, he'd told her, but she didn't need anything more.

Right now, that was enough. Especially when she'd kissed him and the veneer of the lazy playboy had cracked apart completely, leaving a hungry panther in its place.

Oh, she'd wanted him so badly. His heat and his hands on her. Wanted the electricity that danced between them. Wanted his danger, his wicked edge. Wanted his hunger for her to consume him as much as she was consumed by her own.

And it had.

She'd loved him ripping her wedding gown from her and her lacy underwear too. Loved how he'd picked her up in his arms and carried her to the couch, laying her down on it. Loved how he hadn't even stopped to undress, before spreading her thighs, and thrusting deep inside her.

It hadn't hurt. It hadn't even felt strange. It had felt right and perfect, as if he was supposed to be there. As if they were supposed to be joined in this way, a raw, elemental meeting, creating magic between them.

Willow looked up at him, still dazed, meeting his eyes gone gas-flame blue. And she opened her mouth to tell him how amazing he was and how wonderful he'd made her feel, when he pushed himself off her abruptly and stepped out through the double doors that led to the terrace before she could say a word.

Willow blinked, a cold feeling shifting in her gut.

Had he not liked it? Had it been disappointing? Had she been too demanding? Too difficult? She'd forgotten herself since getting on the plane, hadn't she? She was supposed to be much more distant and self-contained, but she'd asked too many questions, had talked too much. And then she'd been demanding when she'd got here too. Had kissed him with too much hunger, been too needy.

You ruined it. Like you always do.

She'd tried that day, years ago. She'd worked hard for the marks she'd managed to get that summer, but school had always been tough for her, because she didn't like to sit still. She'd showed her father that she'd managed to get a B plus in Biology, and she'd thought he'd be pleased. That finally she'd done something right. But he'd told her it wasn't good enough, that he expected better and why hadn't she'd tried harder?

And that was the problem. She'd tried *so* hard and it still hadn't been good enough for him. Nothing she ever did had been good enough for him. So she'd lost her temper. She'd grabbed the photo of her mother that was on his desk, the only one he had of her and which he treasured. She'd ripped it out of its frame and torn it into pieces, because she'd wanted to hurt him as he'd hurt her. His cold veneer had cracked apart then as he'd rushed to the fireplace, futilely trying to grab at the pieces of the photograph. 'No...no...' he'd whispered hoarsely. 'Not that one... It's all I have left...'

She had hurt him. She'd hurt him badly.

Then he'd raised a hand to his head and collapsed.

It had been her temper that had caused the stroke, she had no doubt. If she hadn't ripped up the photograph, he wouldn't have been in such emotional pain and so perhaps wouldn't have collapsed.

Maybe it was the same here. Something had made Achilles leave suddenly, as if he couldn't wait to get away from her, and it was bound to be something she'd done wrong, because she always did something wrong.

Willow slowly got off the couch. Just before she'd felt as if someone had opened up a bottle of champagne inside her, the bubbles fizzing and filling her with effervescence and light. Now she felt raw and bruised and cold.

Perhaps she needed to go and have a shower or something, rather than to follow Achilles.

That's it, run into the forest the way you always do.

When her father had locked her out of the house, she'd always run into the woods around Thornhaven and disappeared into them, going where the trees didn't mind if she was loud or asked too many questions. The silence of the forest calmed her, though it had never made her feel less lonely. She'd used to make up all kinds of friends in the forest, a boy who would play chase with her and fight dragons with her. A boy who became a prince when she got older. She would sometimes be his knight or his friend. Sometimes she would be his princess and sometimes he saved her. Sometimes she saved him.

But he never told her to 'go away'. And he never told her to 'leave me alone'.

Except there were no forests here and running away wouldn't solve anything. She'd learned that the hard way.

The salty evening breeze came through the open double doors, carrying with it the heat of the day, and it wasn't cold. But still Willow shivered. She looked around for something to wrap around herself, since she was still naked, but her gown lay outside on the terrace where Achilles had stripped it from her.

Her veil though was on the tiled floor next to the couch, so she picked it up, shaking out the flowers that had fallen from her hair and wrapping the beautiful gilt lace around her. It wasn't much of a covering, but it was better than nothing.

Then she stepped out onto the terrace.

The sea lapped against the sheer cliffs below, the dark outline of Achilles' tall, broad figure set starkly against the blue sky. He had his back to her, his hands thrust in the pockets of his suit trousers.

He looked so unapproachable, so complete and self-contained that for a second she couldn't bear to disturb him. Her father had hated her doing that, after all. And besides, what did it matter what she'd done to make him walk away?

'If you think that constitutes a wedding night,' he said without turning around, his beautiful voice roughened, 'then you can think again.'

She hadn't made a sound, so she had no idea how he'd known she was there, and for a second she didn't understand what he'd said. Because he wanted more? Was that what he was saying?

'I'm sorry,' she began, her own voice not much better than his. 'I don't know what I did wrong, but I—'

'Why are you sorry?' He turned abruptly, his gaze meeting hers, rooting her to the spot. 'And you didn't do anything wrong.'

Willow tried to find her usual cool, but for some reason it had vanished. There was a hot, burning expression in his eyes, the lines of his perfect face taut. He was so still and yet there was a tension in that stillness; the panther ready either to pounce or to vanish back into the jungle.

She *had* done something wrong, though, hadn't she? He wouldn't have shoved himself off the couch so quickly otherwise, surely?

'But you left.' She clutched the lace of her veil more tightly around her. 'Why? Was it because I was too… d-demanding? I know I'm not—'

He cursed, something low and filthy in Greek, stopping the words in her throat.

Then he moved, crossing the space between them in a lithe, fluid movement that had her heart suddenly racing, making her very acutely aware that the only thing protecting her modesty was a length of hugely expensive lace.

He stopped in front of her, his gaze holding hers. 'It wasn't you, Willow.'

'Then…what?' She searched his face, looking for clues.

'I had plans when it came to you. And those plans

did not include tearing your dress from you and taking you on the couch like a damn animal.' He lifted a hand and thrust it through his hair in an unfamiliar, agitated movement. 'That was not how your first time was supposed to go.' He cursed again, his gaze narrowing. Then he stepped forward, reaching out to her and drawing her close, searching her face. 'Are you all right? Did I hurt you?'

He was so warm, his hands gentle on her hips. But she remembered his intensity, remembered the hunger of his kiss, the raw demand of it. The way he'd thrust inside her without hesitation, possessive and rough.

It shook her with longing right down to her soul.

'No,' she said thickly. 'No, you didn't hurt me.'

He lifted both hands and cupped her face, frowning at her as if he couldn't quite believe her. 'Are you sure?' His thumbs stroked her cheekbones, a gentle, almost tender touch that made Willow shiver. 'You make me so hungry, Diana. And I thought I had better control over myself than that. But apparently not where you are concerned.'

So. He'd lost control and she, the woman who'd never been what anyone, not even her own father, had wanted, had made him lose it.

The cold inside her melted away.

She stared up at him, leaning into his palms and the gentle stroke of his thumbs. 'I don't care. And I lost a little bit of control myself, too, if you must know.'

His gaze was enigmatic, whatever thoughts he had locked securely away behind the walls in his eyes. And she could see those walls. They were metres thick. And of course her insatiable curiosity immediately wanted to know what was behind them, what he was hiding from her, even though she shouldn't.

She shouldn't want to know *anything* about her unexpectedly passionate husband and yet she did. Not that she didn't know things about him already, about his parents and his long dead older brother…

His thumb moved gently on her skin again and her thoughts scattered in a whirl of sparks.

'I'm sorry,' he said. 'I shouldn't have walked away like that. But you surprised me. You shocked me and I thought I was unshockable.'

She blinked. 'But…why?'

His thumbs paused, the look on his face intensifying. 'Because I have never wanted anyone as badly as I wanted you.'

Her pulse gathered speed, the muscular heat of his body warming her straight through. The lace of her veil was scratchy on her skin and she wanted his hands there instead.

And maybe he knew that. Maybe he could see, because one hand on her cheek spread out in a slow movement, sliding down over her jaw and her neck to rest in the hollow of her throat. The tips of his fingers pressed lightly against her pulse, measuring it. Feeling the pace of her desire.

The blue of his eyes had gone the deep, inky black of midnight, and just as dark and mysterious. 'Shall we try that again?' His voice had become darker too, roughened and hungry-sounding. 'Slower this time?'

'I don't need slow.' She was shivering again, leaning into the hard strength of his body. 'I just need you.'

But something in his gaze flared in response and one corner of his beautiful mouth turned up. 'In that case, you shall have me.'

He didn't grab her this time, though. Instead he picked her up in his arms and went into the house, carrying her up the wide staircase and into a bedroom that had windows everywhere facing the sea and a huge white bed.

There was champagne on ice in a bucket near a low white sofa, and glasses on a low table near by. And rose petals glowing like rubies on the sheets.

Achilles laid her on the bed and then he stepped back, pulling his own clothes off until he was as naked as she was. As naked as he'd been that day beside the lake. She couldn't help herself then, shrugging off the lace of her veil and slipping off the bed, going to him.

The sunset poured through the windows, outlining every perfect muscle of him in brilliant gold, and when she put her hands on him he didn't move, allowing her to explore. To touch the wide, muscled plane of his chest and then the hard corrugations of his stomach. The powerful contours of his arms and the lean shape of his waist. His skin was golden and smooth and velvety, and when she pressed her mouth to it he tasted salty and delicious.

His fingers pushed into her hair, cupping the back of her head as she kissed down his chest, her hand stroking lower, finding the hard length of him hot and powerful. She touched him, stroked him, watching the flex and release of his muscles in response to her touch.

He was mesmerising. She wanted to go down on her knees and worship him, but he stopped her, pulling her close instead, his mouth hungry on hers. He didn't let her protest. Instead, he picked her up and carried her to the bed, laying her out on the mattress, then moving over her. He kissed her deeply, making her moan, and then his mouth went lower, to her throat, tasting her skin the way she'd tasted his.

Willow shut her eyes as he kissed down her chest to her breasts, his tongue on her nipple, teasing her. She gasped and arched up, her hands in his hair. 'Yes,' she sighed. 'Achilles.'

The heat of his mouth closed around her nipple, the pressure drawing a moan from her. She sighed again, arching higher. 'More, please, more.'

'If this is you being demanding then you'll have to do better than that, my Diana,' he murmured. 'Perhaps you need some more provocation. Allow me to provide it.' And before she could respond he moved to the other breast, his hot mouth covering her nipple and sucking lightly on it.

Another raw sound escaped her as sensation burst through her in a bright glitter, like sparks against her skin. And, though a reflexive concern rippled through her, she ignored it. Because she'd lost control of herself downstairs and it had been okay. He'd pushed away from her, but it hadn't been her fault.

It was because he wanted her. Who had ever wanted her the way he had?

No one.

So she did nothing as he moved down further, easing her thighs apart. And when his wicked tongue found the beating heart of her, she gave herself up to the sensation completely.

Pleasure glittered in her blood, sparks of electricity winding everywhere as his fingers spread her wider, his tongue exploring deeper. She moaned, arching her back and lifting her hips, forgetting herself. Forgetting herself utterly.

'Scream for me, Diana,' he whispered against her shivering flesh. 'I want to know exactly how much you like me doing this to you.'

All her concerns fell away, everything subsumed by the pleasure he was giving her. By the touch of his fingers and tongue. And then suddenly everything was drawing tight inside her and the climax hit her like an earthquake, and she did scream, his name echoing off the walls around them.

He didn't stop.

She was still shivering and half blind with the effects of her orgasm as he settled himself between her thighs. And when he pushed into her, there was only that sense of perfect rightness. Of a completion she'd only ever found in the woods, where she could be herself and be free.

His body on hers was a glory, the heat of him and the slight prickle of hair. His hardness against her softness. Everything about him different and yet the hunger in his eyes was the same as the hunger in hers.

She lifted her arms around him, arched against him, encouraging him. He slid deeper inside her.

'Every night,' he said in a low, rough voice, the intensity of him shivering through her. 'You and I just like this. Every night. Do you agree?'

She was lost in the pleasure, lost in him. And right in that moment she would have agreed to anything, especially when it concerned more of him.

'Yes,' she said huskily. 'I do.'

It could have been triumph that flickered across his beautiful face. Or it could have been pleasure. It was certainly satisfaction.

Then as he moved there was nothing but pleasure and the long fall that came after it.

Achilles had never spent much time with a lover and so he had nothing to compare being with Willow to. He'd thought they'd probably spend the entire week having sex and sleeping, sharing meals and then more sex, with a couple of swims thrown in for good measure.

He didn't think that there would be more.

After that first day, she wasn't shy and she didn't hold back. She made no secret of her hunger for his touch or that she enjoyed the pleasure he gave her. She was as passionate as he'd thought, the hot coal of that passion igniting every time he was around, which gratified him on basically every level there was.

And as the days passed and they spent them making love on every available surface, or eating delicious food that was brought in and left for them by his staff, or talking about nothing of consequence, he began to realise what he'd already suspected: that the cool, contained woman she'd been back in England was a lie.

That energy he'd sensed in her, bright and fizzing yet locked down, burst to the surface like champagne bubbles in a glass. She wanted to talk to him about a great many subjects and asked questions constantly, wanting to know his opinion and why and how he formed it. One day she wanted to walk around the entire island and hear about all the different kinds of trees and plants that grew on it, so he hired a local to answer her questions, since he didn't know the answers himself. The next day she wanted to explore the beach and the coast, again full of questions, and again he hired another local to answer them.

She liked to argue with him and, since he liked to argue too, they had a great many very vocal disagreements that both of them enjoyed, and which always ended the same way: with both of them naked and him inside her.

Her bright energy was fascinating to him. He'd been a serious, studious child, always with his head in a book, and he'd known that if he'd met her as a boy he would have been just as fascinated with her then as he was now. She would have dragged him from his books, would have taken him off for adventures in the woods, and he would have followed, helpless to do anything else. Drawn by her effervescent spark.

A few days later they were beside the pool built into the cliffside. Willow was naked, lying on her front on the sun lounger. He'd braided her lovely hair into a long plait down her back, weaving flowers into it, because he liked it when there were flowers in her hair. Her long, golden body was divine in the lazy, liquid heat of the late afternoon, her eyes molten as she gazed at him from the pillow on the white linen sun lounger.

She was a goddess like this. His goddess. A possessive thought and one he allowed himself because she *was* his now. In every way.

He leaned over, running a lazy hand down her elegant back, her skin silky and hot and slick with the sunscreen he'd put on it only a couple of minutes earlier.

'You're made for Greece,' he said. 'For sun and good food and sex. How did you ever survive the cold and rain of Yorkshire?'

She arched under his touch like a cat being stroked. It was strange how the electricity that leapt between them hadn't decreased in any way since they'd been together. He would have thought it would, but it hadn't. If anything it had become stronger, a deeper, more intense pull.

It had made him rethink his initial 'separate lives' idea. That maybe, when they returned home, they could spend more time together.

'Oh, it wasn't so bad.' Her voice was husky with sex and sun. 'Dad used to shut me out of the house, so I would always take off into the woods around Thornhaven. I made up a whole lot of friends to have adventures with.'

Achilles frowned as he stroked down her back again. 'He shut you out of the house?'

She sighed. 'Remember that I told you I was difficult? Well, I was. Always asking questions, always wanting his attention. I was demanding and I hated it when he ignored me. I used to throw the most terrible temper tantrums.' Her golden lashes had drifted closed. 'So he'd shut me out of the house and wouldn't let me back inside until I was quiet. It was good in a way. I found the woods didn't care if I had a temper tantrum.'

There was amusement in her voice, but he didn't find it funny. He didn't like the sound of her as a bright, sparky little girl being locked out of the house for being 'difficult'. Because she was curious and passionate and fiery, yes, but he liked those things about her very much. In fact, he shared some of those qualities himself. She was also quick to laugh, quick to apologise, and had a huge amount of empathy. He suspected that she was a woman of deep emotions and perhaps her father hadn't appreciated exactly how deep.

And he knew himself what it felt like to be unappreciated. To be dismissed and rejected. His entire childhood had been that.

'You find that funny?' he asked quietly. 'That your father never wanted you around?'

Her eyes opened and she gazed at him, an expression he couldn't read in her eyes. 'No, it's not funny. But I wasn't what my father wanted. It was my mother who wanted a baby, but she died in a car accident a couple of months after I was born. Dad had to bring me up himself. He was a surgeon and, though he hired lots of nannies to look after me, they all left one after the other because I was a 'handful'. Anyway, Dad had to look after me himself in the end, and his career was severely impacted. I…' She hesitated. 'I ruined his career in a lot of ways.'

There was a note of pain in her voice and he could feel the muscles of her back tensing up. This was distressing for her clearly and no wonder. She'd been told her father hadn't wanted her.

Theos, he knew how that felt. He knew how that felt all too well.

Anger smouldered in his chest, but he fought it down, because this wasn't about him. Instead he followed his instinct and got up to sit on the lounger next to her, put his hands on her beautiful back and stroke her, massage away that tension.

He could feel her resist a second and then she let out a soft breath and relaxed beneath his touch.

'I was a quiet, studious boy,' he said, wanting to give her something more, something to make her feel good about herself rather than bad. 'I know it's hard to believe, but I was all about study and getting good marks. I didn't have many friends, because I didn't really like doing all the stuff other boys did. But I was curious and asked questions too, though I found a lot of answers in my father's library. I think I would have liked you, though.' He massaged out the hard knots he could feel in her upper back. 'I could have answered some of your questions, and you could have dragged me away from my studies to play games in the woods.'

Slowly she turned her head to the side, her muscles now relaxed completely under his hands. 'Quiet and studious? You?'

He smiled. 'I told you it was hard to believe.'

Her lashes drifted closed and her lovely, almost shy smile turned one corner of her mouth. 'When I played in the woods, those friends I made up, they weren't girls. I don't know why, but I always imagined my best friend as a boy. Sometimes he would save me from certain death. And sometimes…sometimes I would save him.'

He'd never thought he needed saving. He didn't think it now. But he could imagine that if there came a time where he did, she would be the woman to do it.

'And did this boy ever become real?' he asked softly. 'Or was he only ever imaginary?'

'No, he was never real.' She sighed. 'Probably a good thing. Dad didn't like having other kids around. Said they were too loud.'

'You and I should have swapped fathers. Mine didn't care about marks or studying. He always wanted me to go shooting and hunting. And fishing. Playing rugby. All the things a proper English boy should like.' All the things that Ulysses had been good at.

She opened her eyes again, flicking him a look. 'And you didn't?'

'Well, I wasn't a proper English boy. I was half Greek. Not that Greek boys prefer reading books any more than English boys do, but certainly I did. Things in books always seemed more exciting.'

She turned her head a little. 'You never went out and explored the woods at Thornhaven?'

Something inside him hardened. He didn't want to talk about his childhood. He didn't want to feel like a ghost here, on his island, with her.

'Not often,' he said, running his fingers down her back again, lightly. 'So what happened with your father? He had a stroke and you became his caregiver, I take it?' He knew that already, because, after all, he'd done his research. But he wanted to hear the story from her.

A shadow passed over her vivid, expressive face. 'Yes. I had to stay with him after I left school, because we had no one else. I took á job in the village cafe, sometimes cleaned people's houses. I couldn't afford to get a job anywhere else, because that would have left Dad without anyone to look after him.'

It sounded like a miserable existence for someone like her. All her bright passion subsumed into looking after one old man, who from the sounds of it hadn't appreciated what he had. Had she had dreams of more? And if so, why had she stayed with a man who didn't deserve her care?

He certainly wouldn't have done the same with his own father.

'Forgive me, Diana,' he said, unable to help being angry on her behalf, 'but your father sounds like he didn't deserve you limiting your life just to look after him.'

Willow looked abruptly away from him, her muscles tightening once more. 'He's my father.'

He shouldn't push her, shouldn't make this personal. But he was angry for her. He didn't like how she'd locked such a vital, beautiful part of herself away and he wanted to know why.

Calmly, he began to knead her muscles, easing her

tension again. 'Fathers have to earn respect just like anyone else. They're not automatically entitled to it. What did your father do to earn yours?'

She was silent. He could feel her tension, could sense her gathering herself to move away from him. But he pressed down a little harder, adding some more pressure, because she seemed to like being touched and being held.

Gradually, very gradually, she began to relax again.

'He didn't do anything to earn it,' she said after a long moment. 'But the stroke was my fault. Or rather, I feel it's my fault.'

That sounded like her.

He kept up the gentle massage. 'Tell me about it.'

'It's nothing.'

'It's something. Tell me.' He didn't pretend it wasn't an order, because sometimes she liked him being authoritative. It gave her something to rebel against, which he knew she liked also.

But apparently not today, because she let out a breath then said, 'He was a surgeon, like I said, and I wanted very much to do something that would make him proud of me. So I spent the whole of my sixteenth year paying attention to my studies. I…wasn't the best at school, but I tried very hard that year, because he liked me to. I got a B plus for Biology in the end, and I was very pleased. And I expected him to be impressed, but…he wasn't.' She turned her head slightly away, as if she didn't want him to see her face. 'He was disappointed I hadn't got an A, told me I needed to work harder and not to bother him for any less than an A minus. I was…furious. I don't know why it hit me so hard that night, it just did. I'd tried so hard for him—I always tried hard for him—but he just wasn't interested.' Her voice had become scratchy. 'I lost my temper. I wanted to hurt him the way he'd hurt me and so I grabbed my mother's picture off his desk and took it out of the frame. And then I ripped it up into pieces.' She didn't look at him, the setting sun gilding her lashes. 'It was very precious to him because it was the only photo he had of her and he'd loved her so much. He'd never got over her death and I knew that. It was my mother who'd wanted a child, not him, but then she died and he ended up with me, and I… I guess I ended up being a reminder of that.' She paused. 'He was so upset about the photo. I'd never seen him get so emotional about anything. And then he…just collapsed. I had to call an ambulance and they took him to hospital. He'd had a fairly serious stroke and, although they told me it wasn't my fault, I…'

'You still blamed yourself,' he finished gently.

Her lashes lowered again, the tension receding from her muscles as he kneaded her shoulder. 'Dad was always telling me I needed to control myself and he was right. I wanted to hurt him and I did.'

But no, he couldn't have her thinking that. Because it wasn't true. The only thing she was guilty of was loving deeply a father who couldn't love her in return. A father who was too busy grieving someone who was gone.

Like you.

No, not like him. Because it was apparent that Willow still cared, while his own heart remained empty. All his caring was gone. He'd used up the final dregs of it the day he'd left Thornhaven.

Achilles gripped her gently and turned her over on her back, so her pain-filled gaze looked straight up into his. She protested a little, trying to turn away, but he put one hand on the side of the lounger, leaning on it as he took her determined chin in his other hand, holding her still.

'Listen to me,' he said flatly. 'Yes, you were angry and yes, you lost your temper. Yes, you wanted to hurt him. But you were only sixteen and you can't take responsibility for his failings. You were his daughter. He should have loved you and accepted you for what you were, not blamed you for what you weren't.'

'But I—'

'No. You're not difficult and you're not a "handful". You're not demanding. And your temper is a beautiful storm. *You* are a beautiful storm, do you understand?' He said the words calmly, clearly, and with all the conviction in him, because they were true and he wanted her to know it. 'You're passionate and curious and you feel things deeply.' He leaned down, holding her chin firmly, and nipped at her bottom lip, making her breath catch. 'You're a goddess, my Diana. A bonfire.' Another nip. 'A solar flare.' He kissed her, taking his time, taking it deep, hot. 'You're stubborn and challenging and I like it.' Another nip, a little harder. 'I like you angry. I like you passionate. I like you wild. I like you the way you are and you don't ever have to be anything else for me.'

She was trembling, her gaze wide and smoky and dark. She didn't say a word, only reaching for him, bringing his mouth down on hers.

But that was all the response he needed, because he could taste her answer in the desperate, hungry kiss that she gave him, as bright and as passionate and as demanding as she was.

And there in the sunset he took the flame that she was and stoked it higher, turned her into a bonfire, a goddess blazing in her glory.

Then he let those flames of hers burn him to the ground too.

CHAPTER EIGHT

WILLOW SAT CURLED UP in the soft leather seat of the jet on the way back to England, reading a book Achilles had bought her on the flora and fauna of the Greek islands. She found it fascinating, but it was getting harder and harder to concentrate because Achilles was lounging in the seat opposite her, long legs outstretched, gazing at her very intently from underneath his long black lashes.

He was planning something, she could tell.

Anticipation coiled inside her, along with a certain heated excitement. She loved it when he looked at her like that, like a very hungry panther looking at his prey.

He'd done that a lot over the previous week in the white villa beside the sea. He'd done a lot of other things too, showing her all about how taking one's time could lead to the most delicious pleasure. Talking with her about any topic she wanted to discuss, his mind a storehouse of seemingly irrelevant yet fascinating facts that he was more than happy to share. Arguing with her—she especially loved that—about inconsequential things which always ended up with them in bed, who was right and who was wrong forgotten. Walking with her over the island and clearly reluctant to do so, yet willing to go along all the same, before taking her back to the villa's small library and going over some of the things they'd seen out on their walk in the pages of the books there.

Sometimes he was quiet, reading or working on his laptop, and then she'd like to sit and watch him, his stillness somehow calming and relaxing.

There was something steady about him in general that she liked, an anchor that kept her from floating away in the worst of the storms. Not that there had been many storms. Passion burned in her—she could feel it—and yet gradually she'd started to realise that it wasn't anything to be afraid of. Not when there was Achilles around to take it, channel it, and make it bloom like a firework in the night.

All the things she'd been afraid of in herself, he liked and actively encouraged.

'I like you wild,' he'd told her that day by the pool, when she'd confessed to him the terrible truth about herself and her temper. And she'd seen nothing but fierce acceptance in his blue eyes. He'd shown her then, with his hands and his mouth, exactly how accepting he was by stoking that wildness in her and letting it rage out of control. Showing her that there was nothing to be scared of, not with him.

You can't go thinking things like that. He might be your lover but he only married you because of a will. This marriage will be over as soon as you have his child, remember?

Oh, yes, she remembered. But that was fine. That was what she'd wanted after all.

'We haven't talked about what's going to happen when we get back to England,' Achilles said suddenly.

Slowly, she lowered her book. 'What do you mean? Aren't we going back to separate lives?'

'That's what we agreed, yes.' He leaned his head on his hand, his elbow resting on the arm of his chair, his long, powerful legs stretched out before him. He looked relaxed and yet the intensity in his eyes made a lie out of it. 'And my child is to be conceived via medical assistance. Though, to be fair, you could already be pregnant.'

A little electric shock pulsed through her. It was true, she could be. They hadn't used anything in the way of protection and to say they'd been having a lot of sex was an understatement.

She looked down at the book in her lap, feeling suddenly self-conscious. She hadn't been thinking about the child he'd wanted, not once while they'd been on Heiros. She hadn't thought about the future at all. She'd been too consumed with him and how he made her feel every time he touched her, smiled at her, laughed with her.

It's just a business arrangement, remember?

No, she hadn't remembered. She'd fulfilled one of his requests and now it was time to fulfil the other. Bear him a son. A little boy with blue eyes just like his...

Something in her chest gave a pulsing ache, an unexpected longing tugging at her deep inside.

She'd always thought children weren't for her, that she wouldn't make a good mother. Her temper was too wild, too volatile. And after what she'd put her father through, the thought that she might lash out at her own child in the same way made that decision a simple one.

And yet, Achilles had told her that she wasn't difficult or demanding. That her temper was a beautiful storm and that he liked it, so perhaps... Perhaps she wouldn't make such a bad mother after all.

But he'd said that their marriage wouldn't be a real one and that their child would stay with him, though she could have access to it.

You really didn't think that one through, did you?

That ache in her chest sank deeper and she found herself clutching the edges of the book. 'So what are you saying?'

He didn't answer for a long moment. Then abruptly he shifted, leaning forward, his hands clasped, his elbows on his knees, the intensity in his face shocking the breath from her. 'I don't want us to have separate lives when we get back to Thornhaven. And I don't want to use medical assistance to conceive. I want us to live together, have a proper marriage.'

Shock pulsed through her. 'A...proper marriage?'

'Yes.' His gaze was like a laser beam boring into her. 'Living together as husband and wife. The same house, the same bed. Shared lives. At least until our child is born. Then we can reassess it.'

Long fingers folded around her heart and squeezed. 'But...that's not what you said earlier.'

'I know. But I've changed my mind. We're good

together, my Diana, and I think you know it. And I don't want to give up what we had on Heiros when we get to England.'

It was strange, all the emotion tangled up inside her. Bright threads of joy and excitement wound around darker threads of uncertainty and doubt.

Because being on honeymoon was one thing but living together was quite another. And then there was the issue of the child…

'You said this was a business arrangement.' She tried to keep her voice level, to not let any of her doubt show in her voice. 'That doesn't sound very…business-like to me.'

His intent gaze narrowed. 'What are you afraid of?'

That he'd bypassed her uncertainty and gone straight to the fear that lay underneath it wasn't surprising. She should have expected it really, because he was extremely observant. And so it was a pity she didn't have an answer.

You know why. You just don't want to admit it.

Willow ignored both the thought and his question. 'What made you change your mind?'

'The honeymoon. You. I don't want this to end.'

'A honeymoon always ends.'

'But the passion doesn't. Sleeping together doesn't.'

'What makes you think it will be the same once we're back in England?' She wasn't even sure why she was protesting. 'And once we have a child?'

He didn't answer immediately, simply staring at her. Then, slowly, he got to his feet and came over to where she sat, putting his hands on the arms of her seat on either side of her, leaning in, caging her with all his powerful, muscular heat.

Her breath caught at his nearness and the way he was looking at her, as if he wanted to ignite her right there in the chair.

'You didn't answer my question,' he said, his voice low and fierce. 'What are you afraid of, Willow?'

She stared up him, her heart beating hard, caught fast as she always was when he revealed the hunger at the heart of him. And it was that hunger she saw in his eyes and his expression. Hunger for her and the raw edge of desperation.

He wanted her to agree, that was what he wanted. And he wanted it desperately.

He'd given her so much over the past week. Shown her what her passion could be like when she wasn't fighting it, when she could be herself and not worry about being demanding or loud or difficult. And she couldn't deny that she very much wanted more of that for herself. She also wanted to give something to him in return.

So what did it matter if she felt a little uncertain and doubtful about continuing what they had on Heiros in England? There hadn't been anything bad about it. No, it had been the opposite. So there was no reason to let those doubts stop her, and there was no reason to be afraid. And after all, it had been a long time since she'd felt as happy as she was when she was with him.

She didn't have to give it up, not yet.

'I'm not afraid,' she said quietly.

'Yes, you were. I could see it in your eyes.'

'I was shocked. That's all.' She lifted a hand and touched the side of his face gently, his skin warm against her fingertips. 'And yes, I want that too.'

Blue fire leapt in his eyes. 'There will be no medical assistance when it comes to conceiving our child.'

'No,' she agreed. 'There won't.'

You want him so very much. It could become a problem.

It could. But she wouldn't let it. She might want him, but it was only sex. And sure, her experience with sex might be severely limited, but she knew her own mind. She knew her heart. And it wasn't involved. So where would be the harm?

'We will conceive our son naturally,' he insisted, as if she'd argued with him. 'You will be in my bed every night.'

There had been times on their honeymoon where he would get oddly intense and demanding like this. It was usually in bed, while they were having sex, and sometimes it felt as if he wanted something from her. Something she didn't understand and didn't know how to give. When that happened, she would open her arms and hold him, give herself up to him, and that would seem to satisfy him in the moment.

But she had the sense that it wasn't quite what he wanted.

His skin was warm beneath her fingertips and she let them trail along the curve of his finely carved mouth. 'I will,' she agreed.

'Do not fight me on this.' His gaze burned. 'I will have what I want.'

'I'm not fighting you, Achilles. I want what you want.'

Finally his gaze flickered, the intense blue glow in his eyes easing. He turned his head, his lips brushing against her palm. 'Good.'

She thought he might lean down and kiss her, but he didn't. Instead, he pushed himself away from her and strode down the length of the jet, taking out his phone and starting into a string of phone calls, pacing as he talked.

He was agitated, that was clear, which was unusual. She was the one who usually paced, not him. Was it going home that was getting to him? The honeymoon ending? What?

She wanted to ask him, but he remained on the phone for the rest of the flight.

They landed in London in the early evening and Willow thought they might stay the night in his city penthouse before returning to Yorkshire in the morning. But it soon became plain that wasn't the plan as he ushered them both into a waiting helicopter for another flight north.

It was raining and gloomy when they finally arrived at Thornhaven, but clearly Achilles' staff had spent a productive week airing out the house and freshening it up in preparation for their arrival.

She wanted some time to explore the manor, or maybe even a half-hour to recover from the journey, but Achilles ushered her straight up the sweeping staircase from the entrance and to the master suite.

It faced the rolling back gardens, the fountains and

the woods, though long curtains in dark blue velvet had been drawn over the windows. A massive four-poster bed stood opposite the windows, freshly made up in white linens with a thick, dark blue velvet quilt thrown over the top.

A fire burned in the fireplace, giving the room a warm glow.

It wasn't Heiros, but it was cosy and welcoming, especially with the late-evening snack that had been prepared and was sitting on the coffee table before the fire, a couple of armchairs standing in front of it.

Achilles didn't seem to be interested in the snack, though.

His agitation hadn't eased since they'd arrived back in the country. If anything it seemed to have got worse.

As a staff member put down the last of their luggage, he paced back and forth in front of the windows, his hands in his pockets, a taut expression on his face.

She recognised that expression. She was tired and it was late, and yet still it made her breath catch.

As the staff member closed the door after him, sure enough, Achilles turned from the windows and came straight for her.

She was standing beside the bed and made no move to evade him as his hands settled on her hips and he drew her hard against his body. There was a strange, feral light in his eyes. Something was wrong.

She didn't want to make his agitation worse, so she didn't push him away, merely leaning into the hard, muscled heat of his torso instead, resting her hands on his chest. 'What do you need?' she asked quietly.

'You.' The word was rough and hard. 'Now.'

It was coming home, wasn't it? Being here, in this house. She wasn't sure how she knew, but she could feel it in the tightness of his muscles and in the hard strength of his grip on her hips. He was so tense.

It wasn't the right time to ask, but she didn't like that tension in him. It made her think that he was in pain, and she didn't like that thought either.

'What's wrong?' she asked.

He bared his teeth in what she thought was supposed to be a smile. 'Nothing. Why would you think anything is wrong?'

'You're very tense and restless. You have been ever since we left Greece.'

His fingers firmed on her hips. 'Well, once you take your clothes off, I won't be tense any more.'

Willow debated giving in, letting him work out whatever was bothering him in the privacy and comfort of that big four-poster bed. But some part of her balked. It wanted to know what the matter was, because this man was different to the quiet, thoughtful man he'd been back on Heiros and it troubled her.

If he was in pain, she wanted to help him. Wasn't that what a wife did for her husband? She helped him when he was in pain and vice versa.

Except you're not a real wife.

No, that was wrong. She *was* a real wife. And she'd agreed that their lives wouldn't be separated. They may not be in love, but if they were going to be sleeping in the same bed and being intimate physically then that didn't mean she couldn't help him out emotionally when that was needed.

'Achilles,' she said quietly, looking up into his face, 'what is it?'

She was very warm and he could smell wild flowers—her scent. And her eyes were as golden bright as the flames in the hearth. There was a crease between her fair brows: she was worried. She was worried about him.

He wanted to tell her that there was nothing to worry about, that he was fine. More than fine. And he'd show her how fine he was, right now in fact, in that bed behind her, the bed where he'd probably been conceived.

But he wasn't fine and he knew it.

The difficulty had started back in Greece, as they'd got on the plane from Athens. Or no, maybe it had started before then, when he'd heard her fears about herself, and he'd told her that she was perfect the way she was. Then he had proved that to her, several times, before lying back on that sun lounger with her in his arms, his hands buried in her hair, realising that he couldn't give this up after the honeymoon was done. And not just couldn't. Wouldn't.

He wanted her in his bed every night. To be able to talk to her whenever he wanted. Argue with her if they were both so inclined. Read books together. Walk in the woods together. Share meals and ideas, and passions.

He'd never had that before with anyone and he couldn't see why he couldn't have it with her. Just until their child was conceived.

The desire for it felt so strong that he hadn't been able to sit still the way he normally would, couldn't put it from his mind to come back to later the way he would with anything else. Couldn't pretend it didn't matter to him, either.

And perhaps that was why he was so agitated about it. That it mattered to him. That he wanted her to say yes and couldn't bear the thought of her refusing.

That was a problem, when he wasn't supposed to care.

He didn't know when it had happened, when she'd crept beneath his guard and got inside him. Got him interested in her opinions, her thoughts, and her feelings. And he *was* interested, that was clear. They mattered to him and they shouldn't.

The whole situation had been exacerbated by coming back to Thornhaven, and the wash of memories that poured in on him every time he stepped over the threshold.

Memories of the sitting room where his mother had walked out without a backward glance, leaving his father standing there white-faced and grief-stricken. And he, standing by the door like the afterthought he'd always been. She hadn't even looked at him; she'd walked right by him as though he weren't even there.

Of the dark hallways he'd used to wander at night, feeling as if he were the ghost and his brother were real. Because there were pictures everywhere of Ulysses and none of him. Ulysses was the only one even worth mentioning, while his father barely had a word to say to him.

Of the room down the end of the other wing, a small room, that was his, because Ulysses' room had been a shrine and no one was allowed to go inside but his father. And how he had used to sit at his desk, throwing himself into his studies, because that was where *he* was real. That was where Ulysses couldn't touch him, because Ulysses had been better at sports and physical pursuits, not school work.

There were days when his own existence had felt precarious, as if if he didn't do something to ground himself in reality then he'd fade like smoke, like a dream his parents had once had. He could feel that sense of fading tugging at him even now. As if the house itself didn't believe he was real, that it wanted him just to disappear.

The replacement son. The spare.

The one who should have died.

He hated this place.

So why bother holding on to it? Why come back here at all? Why bother with all of this marriage nonsense for your inheritance in the first place?

Because he couldn't let it go. If he did, his father would win. His father had wanted him to disappear, to have not been born, and he couldn't have that. He would take his inheritance and he would make it his.

He would force the spirits of this place to acknowledge his existence once and for all.

'Achilles,' Willow murmured and gave a little hiss of pain.

And he realised he was standing there, holding on to her tightly. Too tightly.

Theos, he'd hurt her. What was wrong with him? Why was he letting this house get to him? All of that had happened years ago and he'd made his mark now. He'd forced the entire world to acknowledge his existence and they had. He'd become more than his brother would ever be, richer, more famous, more powerful, more notorious...

Forcing away the agitation took every ounce of strength he had, but he managed it, dropping his hands from her and stepping back.

'I'm sorry, *chriso mou*,' he said. 'I didn't mean to hurt you.'

But she was still frowning, still looking at him with some concern. 'What did you say?'

And he realised he'd spoken the whole thing in Greek. Another slip.

Perhaps it would be better if he slept alone tonight. He didn't want to disturb her and he certainly didn't want to hurt her. He didn't want her asking questions, either, because talking about Ulysses, conjuring up his brother's shade, was the last thing on earth he wanted to do.

So he gritted his teeth, forced himself to smile, to relax as if nothing at all was wrong. 'A slip of the tongue. I was apologising for hurting you.'

She shook her head as if that was negligible. 'You didn't really hurt me. It's okay. But you looked upset.' Her gaze searched his face, sympathy glowing there, as if she knew exactly what he was feeling and why. 'Is there anything I can do?'

It made him feel even more exposed than he already

was, that look. And he didn't want to explain, because this agitation, this desperation was inexplicable. Even the things he could explain, such as Ulysses, he didn't want to.

He didn't want to have this discussion at all.

He was tired, that was the problem. They should have spent the night in London, but he'd wanted to get here. He'd thought being here with her would make a difference and yet it hadn't. Perhaps it would tomorrow. He was no fit company for anyone tonight, though.

'I'm not upset.' He knew he sounded cold, but there was no helping it. 'It might be better if I leave you to sleep alone tonight.' He made himself let her go and turn away, moving over to the door.

'Is it this house?'

Her voice was soft yet the question struck him like a blow, pinning him to the spot, his hand still on the door handle. His heartbeat echoed in his head, a loud pulse of sound. 'What did you say?' he asked, even thought he'd heard the question perfectly well.

There was a long pause and he heard her soft exhalation. 'I know about your brother, Achilles. This house must have…some bad memories for you.'

Electricity crackled the length of his body, his knuckles white where they gripped the door handle.

'How do you know about my brother?' His voice sounded strange in his head.

She met his gaze squarely. 'I did what you told me to do. Some research.'

Of course she would have done some research. The information was there on the internet for anyone to see. The reports of the loving marriage of the Duke of Audley and his beautiful Greek wife. The joy when they had their first child—a son. And then the tragedy of that son's death. The single report about Achilles' birth and then nothing but silence. No one spoke about him healing the hole that Ulysses' death had left in that family. No one spoke about him bringing love back into his parents' lives.

No one spoke about him at all.

Because you don't exist. You never did.

His hand was cold where it gripped the door handle, his knuckles bone white, and he had to force himself to let it go. He should leave, get out while he had a chance, and yet he didn't.

He turned around instead.

Willow stood next to the bed, that terrible sympathetic expression still on her lovely, vivid face. Concern glittered in those beautiful golden eyes, as if she cared about how he felt.

He didn't understand why she would. After all, no one else had. And he didn't understand why she wanted to ask him about his past, either. About his brother.

Sullen anger burned inside him, a healing fire.

'Did you, now?' His voice had turned to ice and he made no attempt to adjust it. She had to learn that the subject of Ulysses was out of bounds. 'Then you'll know that the only reason my parents had me was to replace their dead son. He was the heir, I was the spare. And you might also know that it didn't work. That the disappointment when I turned out to be nothing like my brother essentially meant that I was a living reminder of the fact that he was dead.'

Emotions flickered over Willow's expressive face: sympathy, concern and even a touch of anger. And then she was coming across the space that separated them, and he found he'd taken a step back as if to put some distance between them, the door behind him preventing him from moving any further.

She stopped in front of him, that sympathetic gaze stripping him bare. Seeing his pain. Seeing his anguish. Seeing the lost, lonely boy he'd once been, desperate for love and attention, yet who'd been ignored so completely he'd started to question his own existence.

His heartbeat was drumming in his head, and when she reached out to him he flinched. But she only took his hand and held it gently, the warmth of her touch grounding him, keeping the edges of him solid.

'Come,' she said quietly, and tightened her grip, taking a step towards the fire.

He didn't know why he let her lead him from the door and over to the armchair by the fire. Why he let her push him gently down into the chair. Why he let her open the bottle of wine that was sitting on the coffee table and pour a couple of glasses. Why he let her put one in his hand and wrap his fingers around the stem of the wine glass. Why he damn well let her put some food on a plate and put it on the table beside his chair.

'What are you doing?' He couldn't make himself move.

'Looking after you,' she said matter-of-factly.

Then she grabbed her own glass, set it down on

the floor beside his chair, then knelt at his feet. She put her hands on his knees, leaned forward and rested her chin on them, the sensation of the soft warmth of her body against his legs grounding him even further. She looked at him steadily and the fading feeling dissipated. He had the oddest sense that she made him real, somehow.

'Tell me,' she said quietly.

It wasn't a command; he didn't have to do it. But she was watching him and suddenly he had to get it out, to let someone know that sometimes he felt as if he was disappearing, like he'd been conjured out of the air, a god that vanished if no one worshipped him, if no one saw him. And perhaps if he told her, this desperation, this agitation, would go away.

'Ulysses died when he was fifteen,' he said roughly. 'Meningitis. It was very fast. One minute he had a headache, the next he was dead. I know all of this because my father would tell me about it over and over again, how my brother died and how quickly. How he blamed himself even though there was nothing they could do.' His fingers closed on the stem of his wine glass so tightly it hurt. But the pain grounded him. 'They told me a lot about my brother. What he was like and how loved he was. And how they had me to replace him, but I didn't turn out the way they wanted me to be. They wanted me to be him and I wasn't.'

She watched him, her topaz eyes glowing, no judgement in her face. 'Go on,' she said, as if she knew he hadn't finished, and that there was more, so much more to say.

So he did.

'Nothing I did was good enough. My very existence was like a slap in the face to them. Ulysses liked to shoot and hunt and fish with my father, while I liked to read books and look things up on the internet and play computer games. They had me because they thought I would heal the grief in their hearts. But I didn't. I only made it worse.' For some reason all his muscles had started to relax. Even though remembering all of this and uttering it was painful. But the warmth of her body pressing gently against him, the scent of her winding around him, made it easier somehow. 'My mother left my father eventually. She couldn't stand the grief. Couldn't stand being in this house where memories of Ulysses were. My father didn't want to leave for the same reason. So they separated. My mother didn't even look at me, didn't even say goodbye. She walked right past me as if I weren't even there. I was five.'

Willow's body pressed harder against him, her golden-eyed gaze intent. She didn't speak and she didn't look away, and neither did he.

'Dad completely ignored me,' he went on. 'I tried to make him proud—I was desperate to, you understand. But trying to be what my father wanted only made it more apparent how unlike Ulysses I was. So I worked hard at school, thinking that getting good marks and awards would make him see my worth. Make him see *me*. But they meant nothing to him. He didn't care about marks or awards, or how his son had graduated top of his class. I wasn't Ulysses and that was all that mattered to him.'

Willow's hands spread out on his knees, her fingers pressing down on him as if she knew instinctively that was what he needed; some sensation to make him feel as if he was part of the world. 'So what did you do?'

He picked up his wine glass and drank, tasting nothing, remembering the rage that had burned inside him. 'I got an acceptance from Oxford University years earlier than I should have and I thought that finally this might actually get him to take notice of the son that was right in front of him and not the one who was dead. But he looked at the letter and didn't say a word.' The anger inside him, hot all this time, leapt up again. 'He didn't care. So I yelled at him, told him that he had to stop living in the past, that he had to let Ulysses go. That he had a son right in front of him who was alive and who needed him...' Achilles stopped abruptly, gritting his teeth, hating the memory of how vulnerable he'd been in that moment and how his father had cut him off at the knees. 'But Papa said he had nothing to give to me, that Ulysses had taken it all. And that's when I realised how little I mattered to him. To either of them. They couldn't let him go. My dead brother was more important to them than I was.'

Willow's fingers abruptly dug into his knee, an expression of pain and sorrow flickering over her features. But again, she didn't speak, leaving him space to talk.

'So I left,' he went on, taking another sip of wine. 'I left my father to his grief, because that was better than constantly hoping he would change. That he'd miraculously find he had some love left to give me after all.

So I went to Greece and set about making sure that the world knew who I was, that I was alive and Ulysses was dead. And that everyone would have to deal with it.' Which was what he'd done. He'd made the world acknowledge him, forced it to notice that he existed, and notice it had. Every woman he bedded and every company he helped make a success made him more real.

Willow didn't speak, but he could see the gleam of tears in her eyes, and instantly his heart contracted.

'I'm sorry,' he said roughly. 'I didn't mean to make you cry. That's not what—'

'No.' She shook her head. 'Keep going. It doesn't matter. I'm just sad for you and that's okay.'

Had anyone felt sad for him? Had anyone beyond his teachers noticed the lonely, ignored little boy he'd once been? Who should have been loved and adored by his parents if his older brother hadn't died? Or maybe they saw the truth? That there was nothing in him to love?

The cold wound through him, a creeping frost tugging at the edges of his existence, wanting to pull him apart, so he stared hard at her, stared into her topaz-gold eyes, feeling reality harden around him, anchoring him.

'Dad didn't leave me an inheritance,' Achilles said. 'He left me a final test. He knew I would never marry and settle down, never have a son. That's what he wanted for Ulysses, not me. This was his way of denying me, because he always denied me.' Achilles gritted his teeth. 'Did you know that you were intended for Ulysses? That's why I chose you, Willow. It wasn't because you were intended for me. You were intended for my brother all along.'

CHAPTER NINE

CLEARLY ACHILLES HAD said it expecting some kind of response, though what kind of response he thought he would get, she didn't know.

It didn't matter. He'd chosen her initially because of that agreement between her father and his, and it was that agreement that was important, not for whom she'd originally been intended. Could he even say she'd been intended for Ulysses when she hadn't even been born?

So she only lifted a shoulder and, holding his tortured blue gaze, said, 'So?'

Achilles laughed, a cracked sound devoid of humour. 'So? That's all you have to say?' His face had that taut look to it again, anger burning in his eyes, but now she knew what lay beneath that anger. A raw and agonising wound.

Just as she herself had been rejected by her father, he was a boy who'd never been accepted for himself. Who'd been brought into this world to take someone else's place and then had been rejected because he wasn't that person and could never be that person.

A boy who'd been hurt and hurt deeply by the people

who were supposed to have loved him. She could see the pain that caused, it was there in his eyes, though he tried to cover it with rage. He'd tried to be what they wanted and then, when that hadn't worked, he'd tried to be himself, and that hadn't worked either.

It was all such a terrible situation. His parents had clearly been grief-stricken and had never managed to move past the death of their oldest son, and her heart hurt for them. Yet grief could make people selfish—her father, for example—and it seemed as if it had made Achilles' parents selfish too. And that angered Willow.

They'd had a caring little boy right in front of them. A little boy who only wanted to love them, to heal them, and yet they'd been too mired in grief to notice.

So they'd ignored him.

It hurt her. It caused her actual, physical pain. Because she knew what it was to be ignored by the only people who were supposed to accept you without question. Who were supposed to love you unreservedly. To know that the person that you were wasn't acceptable and that trying to be someone else was your only option.

Her father hadn't much liked the child she was, it was true, but at least he hadn't shut her out as completely as Achilles' parents had. At least he'd acknowledged her existence.

There was a lump in her throat that got worse and worse as Achilles stared at her. And what he was expecting her to do at this news, she didn't know. Perhaps show disgust that he'd married her? That he'd taken his brother's intended? Tell him that she'd rather have married his brother?

'What do you want me to say?' She fought to keep her voice level. She could feel the tension in his muscles beneath her hands; he'd relaxed as he'd told her about his parents, but now he'd tensed again.

'Aren't you appalled at my temerity?' His deep, rich voice had a sharp edge to it, a bitterness that cut like a knife. 'Disgusted by how I deceived you?'

'You didn't deceive me. Perhaps if I'd ever met your brother I might think differently, but I never met him. And I have no feelings about him whatsoever.'

'What a pity.' The words took on a serrated edge. 'You would have loved him. I hear he was a god among men.'

She took a breath, staring at the anger in his eyes, hearing the bitter note in his voice. And with a sudden lurch, she realised something: it wasn't only his parents who hadn't let go of Ulysses. Achilles hadn't either.

Because what was all of this but sibling rivalry? Wanting his dead brother's intended wife. Wanting his house. His inheritance. Wanting the love that should have been his and that had been denied him.

Her heart squeezed tight in her chest and before she could stop herself she said, 'Let him go, Achilles.'

He went very still and she felt the shift in his body, the tension becoming taut as a wound spring. His fingers had gone white around the stem of his glass, the way they'd gone white around the door handle not moments before. His blue eyes burned like a gas flame, staring at her as if he'd never seen her before in his life.

'What do you mean?' he demanded.

'I mean, your brother is gone. You don't need to compete with him.'

His expression hardened. 'I'm not—'

'You are,' she cut him off quietly. 'You're so angry with him, so bitter. You want everything that should have been his, and I get it. I understand why. He took your parents away from you and that must have been awful.'

He said nothing, his face set in forbidding lines.

'But he's dead, Achilles,' she went on gently. 'He was just a boy when he died. And it's not his fault that your parents couldn't see past their grief. It's not your fault either. You deserved better.'

He was so tense, his whole body rigid. 'I didn't get it though, did I?' he bit out.

She slid her hands wide on his thighs, pressing her fingers into the hard muscle beneath the wool of his suit trousers. 'No, and you should have. But like I said, it's not your fault you didn't get it, and it's not Ulysses' fault either. Your parents couldn't see what was staring them right in the face.' She took a soft breath, holding his gaze with hers. 'But I can see. You're an amazing man. You have the most incredible mind and I like the way you take things seriously, no matter how silly they are. You're quiet and contemplative, and you're interested in what people have to say. You're very caring too, though I think you'd prefer it if people didn't know that. But I know that. How can I not? When you've done nothing but care for me since we left for Greece?'

He said nothing, the look on his face intense, a muscle in his jaw leaping.

'I'm sorry your parents couldn't see those things,' she went on, her voice getting huskier. 'I'm sorry they couldn't appreciate what they had in you and it's not fair that they didn't. But…you're not Ulysses, Achilles. And you shouldn't try to be. You have a life and you need to live it for yourself, not to spite him or your parents.'

His expression remained taut. 'You think it's that easy? To just…let go of years of neglect?'

'No, of course not. And I'm a fine one to talk, considering my own childhood. But we both have had people in our lives who haven't moved on from the past, and we know what the consequences of that are.' Her hands closed on his thighs, gripping him hard. 'Don't you want to do things differently? Especially if we have a child?'

He stared at her for a long, endless moment and something passed between them, though she couldn't have said what it was. Then he put the wine down abruptly, leaned forward and hauled her up and into his arms.

She didn't resist him, just as she didn't resist when he shoved his fingers into her hair and pulled her mouth down on his, kissing her hard and deep, as if he had a fever and she was the only medicine that would help him.

A kiss that was desperate and demanded an answer, and so she gave it.

She leaned into him, into the hard muscularity of his

body, wanting to give him what she could, because she could sense the wide, deep, unending hunger of him.

The hunger for a connection he'd been denied.

He wanted someone, she could sense that. Someone who would accept him, who wouldn't ignore him. Who wouldn't neglect him. Someone who would appreciate him not for empty charm and a handsome face, but for who he was underneath that.

She could be that person for him. She wanted to be that person.

She was his wife after all, so who better?

His mouth was hot and hungry and he was kissing her as if he was dying, and all she wanted to do was to save him. So when he bunched up her dress she helped him, shrugging out of it and her underwear too, so she was sitting astride him naked. Then he undid his belt and the zip of his trousers, and she reached for him, taking him hot and hard and smooth in her hands.

'I want you,' he growled against her mouth. 'Put me inside you. Now.'

She shifted, lifting her hips, guiding him to her, feeling him push inside at the same time as she flexed, and they both shuddered with the pleasure of it as he slid deep inside her.

Then they both were still.

His gaze was blue and dark, depthless as the sea. 'Look at me,' he ordered roughly. 'Keep looking at me, Diana.'

And she did, losing herself in his gaze as he began to move, at first slow and gradual, then becoming harder, faster. His hands settled on her hips, gripping her tight, the look on his face intense and hungry, looking at her as if she was his last chance of rescue.

She lifted her hands and cupped his face, kept looking into those depthless blue eyes, losing herself in the rising pleasure and letting him see exactly how it affected her. Letting him see how *he* affected her. And his movements become more insistent, more desperate.

But she didn't look away, and when he slipped a hand between her thighs and stroked her, and the orgasm swelled around her, she let him see her get swept away. And she called his name and felt it when the pleasure came for him too.

Willow lay against him, her head resting on his shoulder, her long, lithe thighs on either side of his, her soft breasts pressing against his chest. Her hair was a wild storm over her shoulders, the silk of it warm against his fingers. He still had one hand buried in the soft, silky skeins.

The orgasm had felt as if someone had taken a cricket bat to his head, making it ring, and he couldn't have moved if his life depended on it. But that didn't seem to matter. She'd looked down into his eyes and he'd felt more real with every thrust of his hips. With every gasp she gave and shudder that shook her lovely body. She'd done exactly what he'd said and hadn't looked away, and it felt as if she'd called him into being.

And now that strange, dissipating feeling at the edges of him had gone.

He felt real and solid and warm and lax. The agitation had gone, as if some poison had been drained out of him and the hollow that had been left in its absence had been filled up with the feel of Willow's body gripping his, her heat and her scent, the sound of his name in her smoky, sexy voice.

Let him go, Achilles...

His hand tightened in her hair. She was right, of course. She was right about all of it, he could see that now, and perhaps part of him had known all along. That in being so obsessed with having everything Ulysses should have had, he'd kept his brother alive. Just as his parents had in many ways.

But his brother wasn't alive. He was gone. And his only crimes were to have been born before Achilles and then to die before him too.

Theos, so much anger over one dead boy. A boy he might even have liked if he'd met him.

And as for his parents, well, maybe she was right. Maybe the fault lay with them and their refusal to give up their grief, rather than a failing in himself.

It was something he'd never know for certain though, since they, like his brother, were dead. All he had left of them was a name and a title, and a house that wasn't even his.

Not yet.

No, not yet. But he would have it. And maybe once he did, he could finally let go.

Achilles ran a hand down Willow's back in a long stroke, her skin damp and warm, and she shivered. Generous, warm woman. No, there would be no separate lives for either of them. She would sleep with him every night, here in this bed, because she was his now, completely and utterly. And if she wasn't pregnant now, she soon would be. He'd make sure of it.

Gathering her in his arms, he left the chair and moved over to the bed.

Then he laid her down on the mattress and stripped off his clothes and claimed her all over again.

CHAPTER TEN

WILLOW LEANED AGAINST the bathroom vanity and took a slow, deep breath. The pregnancy-test kit sat on the smooth marble, the pink lines standing out neon bright on the white strip.

Pregnant. She was pregnant.

She shouldn't feel so shocked, not given how seriously Achilles had taken the task of conception over the past month, and she definitely shouldn't feel a spiralling sense of panic either, not given how she'd known a child was required when she'd signed his contract all those weeks ago.

It just hadn't seemed real then.

It was *very* real now, though.

She and Achilles were in his penthouse apartment near Hyde Park in London—he didn't spend a lot of time at Thornhaven, telling her that he was a busy man and being close to his office in the city was preferable. But she knew it wasn't all about being busy.

He just didn't like being at Thornhaven, which, given what he'd told her about his upbringing after they'd got back from Greece, she could definitely understand. The old house had very bad memories for him, so no wonder he didn't want to be there, and letting those memories go was obviously a struggle. But it did make her question once again why he wanted to keep it so badly. Wanted to so much that he'd married her and now was going to bring a child into the world just so it was his.

But then, it wasn't really about Thornhaven, was it? It was about his brother. About his own neglected childhood. About the pain that she'd hoped to ease in him and yet it seemed as if she hadn't. Of course, that kind of wound wasn't going to magically get better with a bit of conversation and sex, she understood that. It would take time to heal. Time and care.

Time she didn't have. Because now she was pregnant, their marriage would be over. That was what she'd agreed to on the plane from Greece. They would be together until their child was conceived and no longer.

No.

Sudden tears filled her eyes, a bone-deep denial echoing throughout her entire body.

The past four weeks with him had been magical. Just being with him had been magical. During the day he went to work while she was left to her own devices, applying for places at some of her preferred universities, then exploring some of London's beautiful gardens and galleries. At night, when he came home, he would take her out to dinner to fabulous restaurants, where they had a wonderful time in each other's company, before ending up back in bed in the penthouse, their clothes torn off and on the floor more often than not.

It was perfect and she didn't want it to end.

And now all she could think about was how much more perfect it would be if it was just them, and their child. Together.

A real marriage. A real family.

Her heart pulled tight and then something expanded inside her, a ripple of light, a pure, glittering thread.

She knew what it was. It had been sitting there on the edges of her consciousness, just waiting for her to notice, though she'd tried so hard not to.

She couldn't ignore it any more though.

The ripple of light spun harder, filling her, and for a moment Willow resisted, afraid of the intensity, afraid of the depth and strength of the emotion that tugged at her. But she wasn't the Willow so afraid of her own emotions that she tried not to feel anything at all. She wasn't that Willow any more.

She was Diana. The huntress. A warrior and a goddess, who was perfect the way she was, and so she let the light spill through her, become her, burning away her fear, filling up her hungry soul with joy and happiness and strength.

She hadn't thought she wanted love, but here it was. It had found her.

Love for Achilles and his passion. Achilles and his strength, his calm. His arms, his touch, the anchor that kept her from being battered by the storms.

Achilles, and the child she now carried. His child.

She blinked back the tears, but there was no stopping them, the stick blurring on the vanity in front of her. It was pointless to resist. There was no escape.

No trying to tell herself she didn't want it, that she didn't need it.

She did want it and she did need it. She needed it with every fibre of her being.

And their child needed it too.

Would Achilles love this small life as she would? Or had this child ever only been a means to an end? Would their son or daughter grow up knowing that the only reason for their existence was a stipulation in a will? Would they find out somehow that they hadn't been wanted? That an inheritance and a university degree were more important than they were?

Willow's hand crept down to her stomach, her palm pressed there as if to protect the life growing inside her from the harshness of her thoughts.

No. *No.*

A fierce feeling of protectiveness filled her, a certainty that went down to the bedrock of her soul.

Their child would *not* grow up neglected and hurt the way its parents had been. It would *not* feel the pain of not being accepted, of being ignored. It would *not* know what it was like to be unwanted, and she would make sure of that with everything in her.

She'd always thought she wouldn't make a good mother, but the intensity of the emotion in her heart now made her realise that her doubt didn't matter. Neither did her fear.

It was love that was the important part. And it was love that would guide her.

Warm arms snaked suddenly around her waist and she was pulled back against a hard, hot male body. His lips brushed the side of her neck, his breath warm on her skin, and she shivered. 'There you are, Diana,' he murmured. 'I've been looking for you everywhere. The limo is due to arrive in about…' He stopped, his blue gaze meeting hers in the mirror, sharpening. 'You're upset. What's wrong?' There was a note of concern and tenderness in his voice that made her whole soul ache in a way it hadn't before.

Did he feel the same light inside him? He'd never spoken of love beyond that one warning he'd given her, that whatever was between them had to remain purely physical.

But that had been before their honeymoon. Before the four weeks of magic they'd created between them.

He frowned, his gaze searching her face. 'What is it, *chriso mou*? You've gone pale.'

Willow turned around and looked up at him.

He had his tux on for the gala he was taking her to, his black bow tie undone and hanging around his neck. His white shirt was open at the neck, exposing the golden skin of his throat.

The stark black and white of his evening attire highlighted his wide shoulders and strong chest, the dramatic masculine beauty of his face. His eyes were that dark, midnight blue she'd come to love so much.

Yes. Love.

She loved him.

But your marriage will end.

Did it have to, though? Couldn't they go on with what they were doing? They were a family now, and their marriage might as well be a real one, given she and Achilles were already living together. So…why not?

Her heart was full, pushing against her breastbone, and she couldn't speak. Doubt swirled in her head, but she ignored it. This was about more than her fear and what she wanted. This was about what was best for their child.

So she picked up the stick sitting on the vanity and showed him.

Achilles went very still, his gaze zeroing in on the stick. Then he murmured something emphatic under his breath and he shifted his attention from the stick to her. His eyes glowed with something fierce and hot, a possessive kind of look that had the bright, silvery feeling inside her shining. Then he cupped her face between his hands and kissed her hard and long and deep.

Every part of her thrilled to it. To the satisfaction in that kiss and the possession, the fierce taste of his triumph.

Yes. He wants this too.

Achilles lifted his head, his eyes glowing, his beautiful mouth curving in a smile of triumph, and she knew it was true. He wanted this as badly as she did.

'My Diana,' he murmured, nudging her gently up against the vanity. 'I can't think of a more incredible woman than you.'

She put her hands on his chest, smiling up at him, breathless with the most intense happiness. 'It wasn't all me. You had a part in it as well.'

'It's true, I did.' His hands ran down her sides lightly. She wore a golden gown in preparation for the gala that he'd handpicked himself. It was a close-fitting sheath that left her shoulders and arms bare, while the deep vee of the neckline made the most of her décolletage.

'In that case we are both amazing.' He kissed her again, hungrier this time. 'This is exactly what I wanted, *chriso mou*, exactly.'

A family with him. Happiness…

She leaned against his strong chest, loving the heat of him against her. 'I…know we agreed to be together just until the child is conceived, but…' She hesitated a moment, looking up into his eyes. 'We could stay together.'

He frowned a little. 'What do you mean?'

'I mean…perhaps we could stay being married.' She smoothed the white cotton of his shirt over the hard, muscled plane of his chest. 'We could continue living together, being together. We could even raise our child together.' She swallowed. 'We could be a family.'

There was a moment's intense silence and Willow knew instantly she'd said the wrong thing.

'Why?' The word was flat, an iron bar. 'Why would you want that?'

Her hands firmed on his chest as she tried not to respond to the cold note in his voice. 'Well, wouldn't that be best for the child? To have both parents?'

Some of the tension had gone out of him, though the smile he gave her was forced. 'Yes, I suppose that's true.'

'It is, and besides, what if this child is a girl? Would you want to stop trying for a boy?'

'No.' Something hot and fierce glowed in his eyes. 'You really want to stay being my wife, Willow?'

'Yes. Of course I want that.'

He stared at her, his expression suddenly intense and even fiercer. 'A family,' he murmured, as if half to himself. 'Yes, why not? Dad would have hated that.'

And just like that, the bright light inside her dimmed.

Because it wasn't desire for her or for their child that ran through the centre of him, she could sense it in the tension in his muscles, see it in the taut lines of his face.

It was anger. Which meant the past still had him in its grip.

That wound is deeper than you can heal.

No, it was deep, no question. But it wasn't mortal. And she already knew it was going to take time. She could help him with that, she was sure of it.

'Please don't agree just to spite your parents,' she said quietly.

The glow in his eyes focused sharply on her. 'What? What do you mean?'

'I mean, you should have a family because you want one. Because you want a wife and a child. Because you love them.' Her mouth had suddenly gone dry, but she made herself say it. 'A family isn't about gaining an inheritance or getting revenge, Achilles. A family is about love. Or do you want your children to have the same childhood you had?'

She was pushing him, she knew it. And perhaps she'd pushed too far, because the expression on his face shut down and let her go, stepping back.

Her heart shrivelled in her chest at the cold look on his face, her fingers curling around the warmth of his body still lingering on her palms. And she wanted to go to him, tell him she didn't mean to push, that if he didn't want a family then they wouldn't, that as long she could keep being with him she didn't care...

'Are you ready?' His tone was courteous, but she could hear the iron in it. He didn't want to talk about this. 'The limo will be here any moment.'

An ache crept slowly through her. Because this was familiar, the distance in his voice and the cold, hard edge to the words. He sounded exactly like her father, putting her from him as if her emotion offended him.

You shouldn't have said anything.

The ache deepened, part of her wanting to be quiet, to contain herself, do what she'd done all her life and keep herself in check. Yet there was another part, the protective, passionate part, that was urging her to fight for what she wanted, because this was important. It wasn't just about her now, but their child.

And after all, this was Achilles. Who liked her anger and her intensity. Who'd told her that she was a beautiful storm. So why not push him? Why not challenge him? So very few people did...

'Is that it, then?' she demanded, not tempering herself this time. 'Is this how it's going to be? Whenever we have a discussion about what's killing you, you walk away?'

His eyes had gone so cold, his expression a mask, but she went on, 'And what will you tell our child when they want to know how we met? That you married me and conceived them for an inheritance? That they were only ever wanted as a way to get back at your long-dead family?'

Achilles said nothing. He turned his back on her and headed straight for the door.

But that bright thread inside her was hot and it burned, and she wasn't afraid of it, not any more. Not when she had nothing left to lose.

It was a lifeline and so she threw it to him.

'I want you, Achilles,' she said. 'I want to be your wife. I want you to be the father of my children. And I want a family and a life with you, and not because of some stupid will, but because I love you.'

Achilles stilled in the doorway, conscious of his heart giving a strange jolting leap just as it froze solid in his chest

Love. She loved him.

Shock filtered through him. He hadn't thought about love, not for one single second. Love was never supposed to be part of this and, because he hadn't thought of it, some part of him had assumed that she wouldn't either.

He was wrong though, and maybe, on reflection, he should have known this would happen. That she was too passionate a woman not to let her feelings become involved. Then again, he had no reason to think she would love him, not when no one else ever had.

You always wanted it though. You're desperate for it.

Ice swept through him, his breath catching, a deep

pain unfurling inside him, but he shut it down before it could take hold.

No. He didn't need it. He didn't want it. The last time he'd been that desperate he'd been sixteen and his father had told him that he had nothing left to give him. And in that moment Achilles had felt something in his own heart flicker and go out, leaving a void inside him.

It had been a blessing, that void. Because if he didn't feel anything, then there was no pain, and he was sick of pain. Sick of hope. Sick of everything that love brought with it.

He'd been glad that it had gone, and he was in no hurry to reignite that flame.

'You shouldn't have said that.' His voice sounded cold, and he made no attempt to soften it.

'Why not?' Hers, by contrast, was hot, the fire at the core of her blazing in every word. 'Why shouldn't I love you?'

She stood by the vanity in her golden gown. She hadn't got completely ready; her hair was still loose in a wild tangle down her back, and she hadn't yet put her make-up on.

Her eyes glowed like jewels, her vivid, expressive face filled with something light and somehow defiant.

His golden goddess, blazing with strength.

Something flickered inside him, but he crushed it. Suffocated it.

She's offering you everything you always wanted.

Yes, it was true. His beautiful wife was pregnant with his child and now she was in love with him…

But he couldn't take her. He couldn't close that distance between them.

Because now he understood. Now he knew exactly what his father must have felt the night Achilles had confronted him, telling him that he had a son who was alive and who needed him. And Andrew Templeton must have felt this same void where his heart should have been. This same emptiness, right down deep at the core of him.

He had nothing to give her, which meant he couldn't take what she was giving him. If he did, he'd be no better than his father, taking love and never being touched by it. Never giving anything back. Taking it all until Achilles' heart was just as empty and barren as his father's had been.

He couldn't do that to Willow. Not to his beautiful Diana. And not to his child, either.

'You can't love me, because I have nothing to give you, Willow.' He tried to sound level. 'I don't love you.'

Another woman would perhaps have collapsed in floods of tears, or run from the room. Or turned her back on him and pretended nothing was wrong.

Women had all done that to him at various stages.

But Willow did none of those things.

She stepped away from the vanity and strode up to him, the material of her gown shimmering in the light. The look on her face blazed with something fierce, and a deep part of him gloried in how magnificent she was in this moment, even as another part killed that feeling stone dead.

'I don't think that's true.' There was a fierce note

in her voice, a certainty that somehow worked its way inside him, making him ache. 'I think you're lying.'

The ache met the emptiness at the heart of him and died.

'Why would I lie?' He stared at her, let her catch a glimpse of the void. 'I told you that this was only physical. You should have believed me.'

Her gaze searched his, pain glittering in her eyes. 'It's not me you're lying to though, is it? It's yourself.'

'I don't know what you mean.'

'I think you believe you don't love me. I think you believe you don't love what we have, and this baby we conceived. I think you're telling yourself that you feel nothing, when in fact it's the opposite. You feel everything.' Her hand lifted and cupped his cheek and he almost flinched. 'I love you and I want to give you that love. And so will our child. We could—'

He'd taken her wrist in his before he could think straight, pulling her hand away, her touch burning like embers against his cold skin. 'Don't,' he ground out as an inexplicable pain flickered through him. 'Don't touch me.'

She didn't move, her gaze blazing into his. Demanding. Challenging. 'Talk to me. Tell me why you don't want this, Achilles. Tell me why you don't want me when I know you do. When I can see it every time you touch me, every time you're inside me. You look at me like you want something from me and I think I know what it is now. I think you want love.' She flung out her hands. 'Well, here it is. Take it. Or perhaps I'll just give it to you instead. I'll give it *all* to you.'

Of course she would. She would give until there was nothing left of her, until her beautiful heart gave out. She didn't know the truth about love, that you could only give so much. And if she gave it all to him, there would be nothing left for their child.

He couldn't have that. He couldn't have yet another casualty of Ulysses' death.

Achilles let her wrist go and stepped back, taking himself away from the heat of her. Because a void swallowed heat. It crushed it, suffocated it. And he couldn't do that, either.

'You've already given me everything I could possibly want,' he said carefully, wanting to keep the hurt to a minimum. 'It's not your fault, *chriso mou*. It's not your fault I can't give it back.'

She went suddenly still, tears starting in her eyes, as if she knew already what he was about to do. She was perceptive, his Diana.

'No,' she whispered. 'Please, don't.'

But he said it anyway. 'You can live at Thornhaven. When our child is born, and if it's a boy, I'll sign it over to you. If it's a girl, I'll buy another manor for you, one with lots of woods for you to ramble in.' It was the least he could do. Strange how his inheritance now seemed…unimportant, his anger at his father and his brother gone. Perhaps it meant that he'd finally managed to do what she'd tried to help him with weeks ago. Perhaps it meant that he'd finally let go.

'You will receive a generous sum of money every month for you and the child.'

'Achilles, please—'

'The divorce will be quick and painless, I promise. The woods should have always been yours.'

Tears ran down her face, fury blazing in her eyes. 'So you're leaving me? Is that what you're doing? What did I do? Was it me loving you? Was that the difference? Is it my love that you can't handle?'

He couldn't bear the cruelty of a lie, not to her, not about that. 'No. Your love is precious and you should save it for someone who needs it. And our child will need it.'

'And you don't?'

'No. Of course I don't.'

'But…that's not true.' Her face was flushed, tears staining her cheeks. 'You do need it. You want it so badly, Achilles. So why won't you take it?'

That at least had an easy answer.

'Because I can't give it back, *chriso mou*,' he said expressionlessly. 'I told you already. I don't love you. I don't love *anyone*. All the love I had I gave away, and now there's nothing left. Nothing for you or for our child, and I can't have that. I can't have you giving your heart away to another man who won't give you anything back. You deserve more than that, my Diana. So much more.'

Fury flickered in her eyes. 'Oh, that's rubbish. Love doesn't work that way. You wouldn't have spent all this time and energy on marrying me and getting Thornhaven if you really had nothing left, because you wouldn't have cared. You would have sold the house and moved on. But you didn't, did you?'

She's right.

He ignored the thought. 'You don't understand.'

But she hadn't finished. 'Oh, I understand. I understand that you love me, Achilles. You want me and you want our child, and you want us desperately. But you're afraid, and that's the real problem, isn't it? You're too afraid to take what you want and are telling yourself a whole pack of lies instead!'

That pierced the emptiness inside him, letting a hot thread of emotion in, and he'd gripped her, taken her by her upper arms before he knew what he was doing.

'You're wrong,' he said roughly. 'I gave everything I had, everything I was to my parents, and it still wasn't enough for them. They sucked me dry, Willow. And I have nothing left. *Theos*, don't you think I would love you for ever if I had a choice?'

All at once the fury in her gaze turned into something else—anguish and a terrible pity. 'But you do have a choice, don't you see that?' Her voice was hoarse. 'You can choose to stop letting your childhood dictate your own heart to you. You can choose to let that go. You might not choose me, I can understand that. But at least you can choose our baby.' Tears slipped down her cheeks. 'There's always love left, Achilles. It doesn't run out, no matter what you think.'

Dimly, somewhere inside him, there was pain, a brief, flickering agony. 'You're wrong,' he said harshly. 'Because if love didn't run out there would have been some left for me. And there wasn't, Willow. There was nothing at all left for me.'

'Oh…my Achilles…' she whispered brokenly, reaching up to him.

But he let her go and stepped away before she could touch him. Before anything about her could touch him.

Then he turned on his heel and walked out.

CHAPTER ELEVEN

AFTER ACHILLES HAD left for his gala, Willow commandeered his helicopter—because she didn't see why she shouldn't—and got his pilot to take her home, back to Yorkshire.

To get her through the agony of leaving, she gripped onto fury, letting it propel her. She took nothing with her, leaving everything behind, including the beautiful yellow diamond engagement ring he'd given her.

He'd made his choice and so she would make hers, and that was to have nothing of his ever again. The only thing she would take was his child, which was half of herself anyway. It was only fair. He didn't want it anyway, he'd made that abundantly clear.

Except of course that was a lie. Everything he'd told her was a lie. That he didn't want her, that he wasn't desperate for her. That he didn't love her. Because if he hadn't, he wouldn't have pushed her away so completely.

He was afraid, and she understood that, but he should have trusted her. He should have trusted that she had enough love for both of them and for their child too, and that was what hurt the most. That he'd held on to the lie instead of her.

Perhaps she should have stayed and spent weeks trying to change his mind. Or months. Or even years. But she couldn't face spending the rest of her life trying to get another man to change his mind about her the way she had with her father. Achilles had been right about that at least.

As the journey home stretched out before her and her fury gradually began to dissipate, the bright thread in her heart grew sharp blades, cutting her to pieces.

Love made her strong and gave her hope, but it also hurt so much.

She managed not to cry all the way back to her run-down Yorkshire cottage, but once she'd opened the door and stepped into the dark hallway, and the silence closed all around her, she leaned back against the front door and slowly slipped down to sit on the floor, tears falling silently down her cheeks.

He'd told her that it wasn't her fault, but she couldn't get out of her head the sight of his face as he'd told her that if love hadn't run out then there would have been some left for him, and there hadn't been.

He'd been so damaged by his family. So hurt. And he really was beyond her ability to heal. All she could do was push, and if she hadn't pushed, then maybe he wouldn't have pulled away from her. If she hadn't told him she loved him, then perhaps she would even now be on his arm at the gala.

But she had told him. And in the end, that love hadn't been enough for him, the way it hadn't been for her father. At least not enough to change his mind. Or maybe it just wasn't the right kind of love.

Willow lifted her hands and wiped her cheeks as her heart slowly ripped itself to pieces in her chest.

There were only two choices in front of her now: she could go back to London and beg him to take her back, tell him she didn't mean it, that he didn't have to take her love if he didn't want it. They could be together, live together, her loving him and he... Well, who knew what he would do? But that was the kind of life she'd lived with her father, where she was constantly checking herself, constantly fighting the thread of passion that lived inside her.

Or there was the other choice: staying here. And bringing up their child alone.

The thought hurt, it hurt so much. Because she knew there would never be another for her. Achilles would be the only man in her life and perhaps she'd known that the moment she'd seen him coming out of the lake.

It would be lonely, but in the end that was the choice she had to make.

He'd taught her that she was perfect just as she was, even if just as she was had been too much for him in the end. She couldn't go back to who she'd been before. She didn't want to. Not with a child to think of now. A child who needed her. And if Achilles wouldn't let her love him, then she would pour all that love into his son or daughter.

She would be strong for them.

Willow took a shuddering breath, pushed herself to her feet.

And got on with the business of living.

* * *

She was gone by the time he returned from the gala, but he'd expected that.

He sent someone to watch over her, because she was pregnant with his child and he wanted to make sure the pair of them were safe.

He did not go after her. He'd made his choice and he didn't regret it.

He felt nothing and that was a good thing.

Some time passed, he didn't know how long. He'd forgotten to keep track of such things. The member of staff he'd sent to keep track of his wife and unborn child kept him up-to-date with what was happening.

Apparently she was cleaning the cottage from top to bottom. She hadn't touched the money Achilles had sent her, so he doubled it and then got his member of staff to do a survey of the cottage and make any alterations to it that were necessary to make it a warm, safe environment for their child.

He didn't think she would argue with him on that and sure enough she didn't.

He stayed in London working. Eating when his body needed fuel, sleeping when he couldn't keep his eyes open any longer, running when his muscles needed strengthening.

He existed.

Or, at least, he thought he existed. But sometimes he'd sit in his office and the city would sparkle in the sunlight, and he felt like a shell of his former self. A shadow. Thin around the edges, mere vapour in the air that the slightest breath would scatter.

A man with a void at the heart of him.

It was a feeling he'd only ever had at Thornhaven, where he was nothing and no one. It shouldn't happen here, in his office, the sun around which the solar system of his company revolved.

More time passed and the feeling worsened. There were days where he felt as if the emptiness inside him might swallow him whole.

The only thing that helped were the daily updates from Yorkshire, keeping him informed of what his wife was doing. For whole minutes at a time he sat reading those emails over and over, feeling himself solidify and become real.

He wasn't sure why that was, and really he needed to stop reading them, because they didn't concern him, not any more. But he couldn't help himself. Couldn't stop imagining Willow, filling up that cottage with her warm, bright presence. Couldn't stop thinking about her passion and fire, her laughter and joy.

And he couldn't stop reading those emails.

Then one day the email came with an attachment. A picture of an ultrasound examination. A picture of their baby.

He stared at it, shocked. Had so much time really passed?

You let it pass. And you did nothing. You sat here in your office pretending you felt nothing. Missing out on precious moments with the woman who loves you. The woman who is carrying your child. Your family. Lying to yourself over and over again...

Achilles shoved back his chair and got up from his

desk, pain filtering through him, turning into a sudden unbelievable agony. It hurt so much he couldn't sit still, pacing to the windows and then back again.

It lit him up like a torch and he had no idea where it had come from.

He was supposed to feel nothing. He was empty inside, a hollow shell. A void. And yet…there was pain. Pain for what he was missing. Pain for what he'd done. Pain for the future he'd denied himself. Pain for the woman he'd turned away.

He tried to tune it out, tried to ignore it the way he always did, telling himself it didn't exist. Because how could it? Pain meant he cared and he didn't care. He didn't care about anything.

Yet as soon as he did that he felt himself begin to disappear, the terrible feeling of not quite existing filling him.

Because it's a lie and you know it.

Achilles stopped by the window, the thought echoing in his head, along with the memory of Willow's voice and the anger in it.

'You love me, Achilles. You want me and you want our child, and you want us desperately. But you're afraid, and that's the real problem, isn't it? You're too afraid to take what you want and are telling yourself a whole pack of lies instead!'

He took a breath, staring outside but not seeing. Was she right? Was the emptiness inside himself, that terrible void, just a lie? A lie he held on to simply because he was afraid?

It's true and you know it.

He took a breath and then another, the knowledge sitting inside of him all this time, a truth he hadn't wanted to see.

Yes, he *was* afraid, so terribly, deathly afraid. Because if the lie was true, if love truly didn't run out, then why hadn't he been given any? Why hadn't his parents loved him? Was it really because he wasn't Ulysses? Or did it go deeper?

Was it him?

He closed his eyes, the pain running like a fault line through the centre of him. It had always been easier to tell himself that he couldn't feel. That love wasn't something he could give. That it was easier to be angry with his father and the brother he'd never met. Easier to blame them than to think it was something in himself.

Something that meant they could never love him.

He would never know the answer to that now, though. They were gone.

You have to let them go.

The pain fractured inside him, and for some reason all he could see was Willow in the bathroom the night of the gala. Willow standing tall and fierce. The light that filled her as she'd told him she loved him. The tears on her cheeks and the pain in her eyes as he'd told her he didn't want it.

Let your parents go. Hold on to her instead.

He froze, every part of him going quiet and still.

She had given him everything. She had never turned him away. Never told him that she had nothing for him. She had opened her heart, had let him give her all his anger and his pain. Had given him hers, too, without hesitation...

Nothing about her had caused him pain except her loss.

Theos, why had he sent her away? Why had he been so afraid?

There was a roaring in his ears, the lie he'd told himself all his life giving way and revealing the truth. The same truth she'd given him in the bathroom weeks ago.

It wasn't that he didn't care. He did care. About everything. And most especially about her. He loved her. He'd loved her from the moment he'd seen her watching him at the lake. And he wanted the life they could have together, the family he could create with her. And he wanted it desperately.

He stood there before the windows, his heartbeat thudding in his ears, fighting to breathe, knowing that he couldn't go on. That he couldn't keep clinging to the lie, continuing to pretend that he felt nothing, that his heart was dead inside him. Continue with this half-life, this bare existence, because that was what it was. That was *all* it was. Just existence.

If he wanted more, he had to be brave like she was. Passionate like she was. He had to step out of the shadow of his fear, let go of the lie, and believe in something else.

He had to believe in her. She'd found something in him to love and he had to trust that. Trust her. Trust the love that was in his own heart too.

He had to, otherwise what else was there?

Only existing. And existing wasn't living.

His hands were shaking as he got out his phone, but he didn't hesitate as he ordered his helicopter.

He had one last trip to make.

CHAPTER TWELVE

WILLOW HAD GONE out blackberry-picking in the woods near Thornhaven. The last of the berries were still on the bushes and she had thoughts of making a pie. The morning sickness she'd experienced over the first eight weeks was starting to ease and she had a sudden and intense craving for the tart sweetness of apples and blackberries.

It was a beautiful day, still and hot, and the woods were silent and cool.

She didn't go too near Thornhaven these days—it hurt too much, made her see things that weren't there, such as a tall man with black hair and eyes like a midnight sky. A man whose passion had taught her soul to sing.

She hated those visions. Because they were never true and they only ended up causing her pain, and so she left the area alone completely.

Just as Achilles had left her alone.

She hadn't heard from him since he'd walked out of his penthouse a month ago and she was furious about it. Not for herself, but for the baby she carried.

He might believe he had nothing to give her, but to continue to believe that when it came to his child made her furious.

Everything about him made her furious.

In fact it was better not to think about him, because she only ended up miserable, and she wasn't going to be miserable. She absolutely refused.

She was passing by the lake when she heard the sound of splashing, and instantly she was months in the past, watching a man swimming naked. Watching him rise from the water like Neptune from the waves, a water god made flesh and just for her.

Achilles...

Her eyes filled with tears and she didn't want to look, because she would only be disappointed. And the disappointment would be so bitter.

But she couldn't stop herself from moving over to the edge and taking a glimpse through the trees...

And her heart caught hard in her chest as a man pulled himself out of the water.

A beautiful man.

Her man.

She could barely see through the tears in her eyes, a sob catching in her throat.

He was here and she didn't know why. He was here, swimming in the lake, so close and yet so far. And how dared he? How dared he come to where he must know she walked? How dared he flaunt himself like this?

And how dared she still love him when all he'd done was hurt her?

She turned away from the sight of him, walking

quickly along the path, blind with tears, when a voice from behind her said, 'Diana.'

Tears were streaming down her cheeks. That voice, that beautiful voice…

'That's not my name,' she said hoarsely, not sure why she wasn't running, getting as far away from him as she could.

'I know.' Beneath the deep, lilting timbre was a note of desperation. Of pain. 'It's Willow. *My* Willow.'

She shook her head. 'I'm nobody's Willow.'

She didn't hear his footsteps, but suddenly there were hands on her hips, holding her tight, pulling her back against a hot, hard male body, still damp from the water. 'Yes, you are.' His mouth was by her ear, his breath hot on her skin. 'You're mine. I claimed you. You're *my* Willow and you were mine the moment I laid eyes on you.'

The tears wouldn't stop, pain and fury building in her heart, and she let them. Because this was who she was. A woman of deep passions. Passions he didn't want, and so what did it matter if she held them back? What did it matter if she let them out?

He hadn't wanted her back in London, so why would he want her now?

She turned in his arms, curling her hands into fists, hitting him on his damp, bare chest, wanting to hurt him for what he'd done to her and to their child.

'I hate you,' she said thickly. 'I hate you so much.'

He only caught her fists in his and gathered them together, bringing them to his mouth and kissing her knuckles. His eyes were very dark, almost black.

'I'm sorry, *chriso mou*,' he said in a low, rough voice. 'I'm so very sorry for hurting you. And you have every right to be angry. Take it out on me, my Diana. You can hurt me; I deserve it.'

His heat took all the strength from her. All she could do was look up into his beautiful, beloved face. 'Why?' Her voice was hoarse and broken. 'What are you doing here?'

'I hoped my swimming would bring you to me.' He cupped her face between his palms. 'Because I've come back to claim what is mine. You. You and our child.'

'I don't understand. You didn't want me. You told me—'

'I know.' His voice was very calm, very sure. 'But you were right about me. And I was so very wrong.'

Willow swallowed, her heart slowing, catching. 'What do you mean?'

'I told myself that I had nothing to give you, that I didn't love you. That I felt nothing at all. I'd convinced myself of it so completely that nothing could have changed my mind. And that's where you were right. I clung to that belief because I was afraid.' There was a hot glow in his eyes, a deep remembered pain. 'My father told me he had no love left to give, that he'd given it all to Ulysses. And I believed him. I had to believe him. Because if I didn't, if there was still love inside him, then why hadn't he given it to me?' His thumbs moved on her cheeks, stroking gently. 'It was easier to tell myself that it was his fault, Ulysses' fault. To tell myself I felt nothing than to believe there was something wrong with me.'

'Oh, Achilles,' she whispered brokenly, her heart aching for him. 'There's nothing wrong with you. Nothing at all. If you believe nothing else, then believe that.'

His midnight eyes stared down into hers. 'That's why I'm here, Willow. Because you sent me that ultrasound picture of our child and all I could think about was what was I missing out on and what I really wanted. And you were right, my Diana. It's you. It's our child. It's our family. That's what I want. That's what I *always* wanted.'

She swallowed, her chest tight, her voice stuck in her throat. 'Achilles...what are you saying?'

'I'm saying that I love you, Willow. I've loved you since the moment I saw you. And I can't be afraid of that pain any more, *chriso mou*. I can't.' His expression became suddenly fierce. 'I've been half-alive for so long. Existing but not living. Holding on to the ghosts of my father and brother, and I can't do it any more. I don't want to. What I want is to love you. Love you until there's no more love in me left to give.'

All her anger vanished. Just dried up and blew away, taking all the pain along with it.

'You idiot,' she said, her voice having gone scratchy and tight. 'You can't run out of love. It doesn't work that way, I told you. The more love you give, the more you have, don't you know that?'

He smiled, damn him. That beautiful, slow-dawning smile that she loved so much. 'No,' he said. 'I don't know that. But maybe you can teach me?'

She'd always been a woman of deep passions and

those passions were strong and true. Her anger was a storm and storms passed, and so had hers, leaving nothing but the one passion in her life that would never change, never flicker or fade.

Her love for him.

So she gave him the only answer she had, an answer that mere words weren't enough for.

She reached up, pulled his mouth down on hers, and started teaching him right there and then.

EPILOGUE

ACHILLES INSISTED THEY renew their vows on Heiros during the university summer break, so there would be no disruption for Willow's degree, and she agreed. She wore a gown of her choosing, very Greek, a chiton of draped white silk and a golden tie at her waist. Her hair was loose and woven with wild flowers.

He had never seen anything so beautiful.

Their son, a golden-eyed terror called Alessandro, caused havoc by the water's edge during the ceremony, and Achilles had to quell him by lifting him up in his arms and making him help him say his vows.

Even Willow's father—who'd surprised everyone by deciding to attend at the last minute—agreed that it was the most beautiful renewal.

Willow somewhat mischievously had suggested they honeymoon in Thornhaven, since their first honeymoon had been on Heiros, but, since the weather was better in Greece, they stayed in Greece.

But it wasn't until deep in the night, after their passion was spent, that Achilles brought out the letter Jane had sent him, which had arrived the morning they'd left England. A letter he hadn't known what to do with and had successfully pushed to the back of his mind until now.

Willow lay wrapped in a sheet, the moonlight shining on her bare silky skin, frowning as she read it. And then, once she was done, she put it down and looked at him, sympathy and pain and love glowing in her eyes.

The letter was written in a shaky hand:

Achilles,
I've been a dreadful father to you and I know that. I wish things had been different, but if there's one certainty in life it's that you can't change the past. I should have moved on, I should have let Ulysses go, but I couldn't. And now it's too late. But it's not too late for you. To that end, I've decided on something that you may think is a punishment, but is not intended as such.

I want you to have Thornhaven, but in order to keep it you must marry and have a son. This house needs a family. It needs children and laughter and happiness. It has been a house for ghosts for too long.

You need a family too. You need to have the family that your mother and I failed to give you. And with any luck, when you do, you will make more of it than we did...

'Where did this come from?' Willow asked, a tear slipping down her cheek.

'Jane found it in amongst some papers in Papa's

study.' He looked down at it, the same pain and love that were in his Willow's eyes in his own heart too, along with a deep regret. 'It seems I was wrong about him. He did have something left for me after all.'

His beautiful wife reached out and touched his face, and just like that the pain inside him was gone, leaving behind it only a bittersweet regret. 'You see?' she said softly, her mouth curving in a smile. 'It never runs out completely.'

He smiled, the emptiness inside him, the void that had been there for so long only a memory. Because now his heart was full, with his wife and his son, with the family they would have and the future they were building together.

With love, of which he had an inexhaustible supply.

Because, as it turned out, his wife was right about that too.

Love really was infinite.

* * * * *

WE HOPE YOU ENJOYED
THIS BOOK FROM

HARLEQUIN
PRESENTS

Escape to exotic locations where passion knows no bounds.

Welcome to the glamorous lives of royals and billionaires, where passion knows no bounds. Be swept into a world of luxury, wealth and exotic locations.

8 NEW BOOKS AVAILABLE EVERY MONTH!

#3901 BRIDE BEHIND THE DESERT VEIL
The Marchetti Dynasty
by Abby Green

After surrendering to passion with a mystery woman, Sharif Marchetti must erase their desert encounter from his memory. Until they meet again...as he lifts the veil of his convenient wife!

#3902 THE ITALIAN'S FORBIDDEN VIRGIN
Those Notorious Romanos
by Carol Marinelli

Italian tycoon Gian de Luca knows Ariana Romano is off-limits. She's his mentor's daughter, and her drama queen reputation precedes her. But when he offers her comfort one night, he's shocked to discover she's a virgin. Perhaps he's been wrong about her all along...

#3903 HIS STOLEN INNOCENT'S VOW
The Queen's Guard
by Marcella Bell

For billionaire Drake Andros, only marriage and an heir from Helene d'Tierrza will recover what was stolen from him. Their chemistry may persuade her to help him, but her vow of innocence may complicate his plan...

#3904 ONE HOT NEW YORK NIGHT
Wanted: A Billionaire
by Melanie Milburne

A sizzling night of passion is exactly what Zoey Brackenfield needs. And since it's with Finn O'Connell, business rival and notorious playboy, there's zero chance of heartbreak. That is, until she starts craving his exhilarating touch...

YOU CAN FIND MORE INFORMATION ON UPCOMING HARLEQUIN TITLES, FREE EXCERPTS AND MORE AT HARLEQUIN.COM.

HPCNMRB0321

"I can't," she repeated, her voice low and earnest. "I can't, because
when I went to him as he lay dying, I looked him in his eyes and
swore to him that the d'Tierrza line would end with me, that there
would be no d'Tierrza children to inherit the lands or title and
that I would see to it that the family name was wiped from the
face of the earth so that everything he had ever worked for, or
cared about, was lost to history, the legacy he cared so much about
nothing but dust. I swore to him that I would never marry and
never have children, that not a trace of his legacy would be left
on this planet."

For a moment, there was a pause, as if the room itself had
sucked in a hiss of irritation. The muscles in his neck tensed, then
flexed, though he remained otherwise motionless. He blinked as if
in slow motion, the movement a sigh, carrying something much
deeper than frustration, though no sound came out. Hel's chest
squeezed as she merely observed him. She felt like she'd let him
down in some monumental way, though they'd only just become
reacquainted. She struggled to understand why the sensation was
so familiar until she recognized the experience of being in the
presence of her father.

Then he opened his eyes again, and instead of the cold green disdain her heart expected, they still burned that fascinating warm brown—a heat that was a steady home fire, as comforting as the imaginary family she'd dreamed up as a child—and all of the taut disappointment in the air was gone.

Her vow was a hiccup in his plans. That he had a low tolerance for hiccups was becoming clear. How she knew any of this when he had revealed so little in his reaction, and her mind only now offered up hazy memories of him as a young man, she didn't know.

She offered a shrug and an airy laugh in consolation, mildly embarrassed about the whole thing though she was simultaneously unsure as to exactly why. "Otherwise, you know, I'd be all in. Despite the whole abduction…" Her cheeks were hot, likely bright pink, but it couldn't be helped, so she made the joke anyway, despite the risk that it might bring his eyes to her face, that it might mean their gazes locked again and he stole her breath again.

Of course, that was what happened. And then there was that smile again, the one that said he knew all about the strange, mesmerizing power he had over her, and it pleased him.

Whether he was the kind of man who used his power for good or evil had yet to be determined.

Either way, beneath that infuriating smile, deep in his endless brown eyes, was the sharp attunement of a predator locked on its target. "Give me a week." His face may not have changed, but his voice gave him away, a trace of hoarseness, as if his sails had been slashed and the wind slipped through them, threaded it, a strange hint of something Hel might have described as desperation…if it had come from anyone other than him.

"What?" she asked.

"Give me a week to change your mind."

Don't miss
His Stolen Innocent's Vow.
Available April 2021 wherever
Harlequin Presents books and ebooks are sold.

Harlequin.com

HPEXP0321